NEW UNDER THE SUN

NEW UNDER THE SUN

NANCY KRESS

COMPANION NOVELETTE BY
THERESE PIECZYNSKI

THE STELLAR GUILD SERIES
TEAM-UPS WITH BESTSELLING AUTHORS

MIKE RESNICK
SERIES EDITOR

an imprint of

ARC
MANOR
Rockville, Maryland

Series edited by Mike Resnick.

ISBN: 978-1-61242-123-0

www.PhoenixPick.com
Great Science Fiction & Fantasy
Free Ebook every month

Published by Phoenix Pick
an imprint of Arc Manor
P. O. Box 10339
Rockville, MD 20849-0339
www.ArcManor.com

CONTENTS

A Greeting From the Series Editor

Welcome to another Stellar Guild book, the ultimate pay-it-forward science fiction series. Most of the field's superstars can't pay back the people who helped them when they were starting out; those people are rich, or dead, or both. So, in this field more than in any other, it has become an honored tradition to pay forward.

The Stellar Guild was created for just that purpose. Each book in the series consists of a novella by one of the field's superstars, plus a novelette by a protégé of the star's own choosing, said novelette being a sequel, a prequel, or a companion piece to the star's novella.

The first four books in the series have been by Kevin J. Anderson, Mercedes Lackey, Harry Turtledove, and Robert Silverberg—and, of course, their protégés. For this fifth book, our superstar is Nancy Kress—multiple Hugo winner, multiple Nebula winner, Campbell Memorial Award winner, Sturgeon Award winner, Clarion instructor, Taos Toolbox workshop leader, Writer's Digest columnist, and the list goes on and on. Nancy's selected protégé is Therese Pieczysnki, and I think you'll find yourself agreeing that she made a fine choice.

And keep an eye out for the next two Stellar Guild books, *Red Tide* by Larry Niven and his protégés (he has two of them!), and *The Aethers of Mars* by Eric Flint and his protégé.

Mike Resnick

NEW UNDER THE SUN

Book One
ANNABEL LEE

NANCY KRESS

Much thanks to Dr. Maura Glynn-Thami, who offered so much helpful medical advice on this manuscript.

♈

"The most beautiful and deepest experience a man can have is the sense of the mysterious. It is the underlying principle of religion as well as all serious endeavor in art and science."

— *Albert Einstein*

I: August, 2013

HANNAH HAD BEEN TRYING to get a signal for an hour now, any kind of signal—cell, Internet, radio, it didn't matter. But she was maybe a hundred miles from civilization and even the effing satellites thought this place was too boring to connect to. This had to be the lamest vacation ever.

Petulantly she tossed her phone onto the scraggly grass and colorful wildflowers of the mountain meadow. Arms wrapped around her long coltish legs and her head on her knees, she stared out over the valley below, where her clueless parents had pitched camp. *The lamest.*

A hawk circled overhead, riding the thermals of the clean blue sky.

So what? It was only a effing *bird.* Mom and Dad could go all literary-rapturous over birds and mountain views and a "pure" mountain spring next to a tent with no electricity or connections, but Hannah had hated every second of this trip and she planned to go on hating all the seconds that were still to come. She wanted her friends and city lights and fun things to do, and all this fake-pioneer stuff without so much as the relief of a cell connection was just—

Where was Annabel?

Hannah jumped to her feet and whirled around. Annabel had been here just a minute ago, she'd been chasing a butterfly across the mountain meadow, it was only a minute ago—

"Annabel!" Hannah yelled, and the mountain gave back the echo: *ANNABEL Annabel Annabel...*

Hannah's belly went cold. She rushed to where she'd seen her little sister chasing the butterfly, toward the cliff face rising up from the north edge of the meadow. Annabel had been barefoot : *"I want empty feet like bunnies,"* she'd said, and Hannah, rolling her eyes, had shrugged and said, "Whatever." But now there were no bunnies, no butterflies, no Annabel. Oh God, *where?*

"Annabel! Answer me!"

ME me me....

Hannah started to shake and sob, running back and forth across the rough grass, searching and calling and running, she was supposed to be watching Annabel oh dear God just let her be all right and I'll never bitch about anything again...

"Hannah!" called a faint voice from under her feet.

She dropped to her knees. A narrow jagged slit in the ground, about a foot wide, one thick plate of rock above and one below. Hannah got flat onto her belly and peered into blackness. She thrust her hand in and encountered only stone. The crevasse sloped away at a forty-five degree angle, deep enough that she couldn't even see Annabel.

"Get me out!" came from the rock. And then, "I'm slipping!" And then nothing at all.

Warm. Warmth touched the cysts. They had not been warm for hundreds of years. Warm, so warm...the cysts' tough outer coating began to dissolve and the life within to stir after its long dormancy.

Drilling equipment had to be brought up the mountain. Before that, Hannah's father had to drive down to the nearest place with phone coverage, the SUV hurtling at terrible speeds down the steep mountain road. Before that, he'd had to run down from camp to the last place the SUV had been able to reach. Hannah's mother stayed at the edge of the narrow crevasse, talking desperately to Annabel. "It's going to be all right, baby, we'll get you out, I promise we'll get you out, help is coming, just a little while longer..."

There was no answer until the rescue team arrived, grim-faced and heavily laden. They snaked an oxygen line down to Annabel, followed by a microphone. Then everyone above could hear her childish wail, amplified and made eerily robotic by the surrounding rock: "I wanna get out!"

"I know, baby, I know, we'll get you out, I promise...."

Floodlights on the meadow, heaters, heavy machinery crushing the wildflowers. More lines went down into the hole: heat, a camera that showed the top of Annabel's head. Sound sensors showed her wedged in a sharply angled crevasse beneath two feet of solid rock, a quarter kilometer above a small mass of twisted metal. That was probably remnants of nineteenth-century mining equipment, although no one had been able to find records of any mine shafts here. The metal was not important, neither help nor hindrance in getting the child out.

Hannah, her guts twisted with fear and guilt, found Annabel's sneakers and little white socks in a heap. Hannah collapsed onto the ground, sobbing, but no one had any time for her.

Warm. Yes. Although not as warm as it had been a short time ago. A host? Yes, if modifications were made. And warm.

The tiny organisms shed the rest of their cyst coverings. The warmth accelerated their chemical signaling, making them collectively so much more than was each alone. They burrowed inward.

"My feet feel funny," Annabel said.

Hannah's mother glanced fearfully at the doctor sitting next to her on a tarp beside the mouth of the crevasse. Around them drilling equipment screamed, breaking up rock slowly, delicately. "It's important that we not do anything that would knock her further down," the chief engineer had explained.

The doctor chose her words carefully. These parents were both, understandably, overwrought. The father blustered and raged; the mother wept. "Hypothermia, most likely. But the heat lamp they snaked down there will prevent any real damage."

"The lamp can only reach as far as her shoulders! They block the rest of her body!"

The doctor didn't answer. She eyed the mother's fingernails, torn and bloody from scrabbling at the rock before equipment arrived. Finally the doctor said the only thing she could say: "Keep talking to her."

Strangeness. The right temperature, but such a different host. Carbon-based, yes, and with recognizable cells and chemical composition, but a completely foreign and unusable genetic system. Desperately the organisms began to reform, trying to conform to the environment, as they had so many times before, on so many other worlds. But such a strange host, where were useful tissues...

Some organisms died. Some reconfigured, working against time and the host's vicious attack cells. Some swapped reproductive information, trying to find an optimum combination for survival. All such activity drastically lessened the energy available for chemical signaling. The environment destroyed nearly all of the signal chemicals.

The organism, scattered and diminished, fought to survive in the alien host.

Hannah's mother told stories to Annabel. She sang until her voice was hoarse, all of Annabel's favorites: "Itsy Bitsy Spider" and "Frog Went A-Courting" and "Soon It's Gonna Rain." Hannah's father argued with the rescue director from the U.S. Mine Safety Administration, shouted orders that no one listened to, and spoke to the TV and Internet cameras kept at the far edge of the meadow by a cordon of police.

"They're drilling a parallel shaft to the one Annabel is trapped in," Hannah's father said, repeating what the rescue director had already told the reporters. They listened anyway, filming his haggard, blustering face. "She's about twenty-seven inches down, and once they get below her, they'll drill a horizontal drift over to her. They're not using robotic drills because human operators can better judge how to use the jackhammers. They're going down about an inch per hour but—"

Hannah wasn't listening, even though she could hear her father's angry shouts over the equipment. Hear her father and mother argue night after night, smell the diesel fuel and wet rock and turned-up earth, feel the hard ground under her in the tent where she lay. The only thing she could not do was see. Her eyes were squeezed shut because if she couldn't see Annabel, if she didn't see Annabel come up alive and okay, she never wanted to see anything again.

By the second day, Annabel had ceased to respond to her mother, not even with whimpers. Hannah's mother was so hoarse that all she could do was gasp into the mic, "Breathe, Annabel, *breathe...*"

The host was weakening. Its central unit sounded slower and slower. The organism didn't know enough to repair the central unit, especially not in the organism's scattered state. But a few of its cells had at last found a mass of tissue where it could feed and rest and, most important, hide from the immune system. The host must live! Because now the organism had no chance of getting back to a place where it could again form cysts. And there had never been any point in getting back to the damaged ship.

"She's coming up!" someone shouted.

Hannah bolted from her tent. A flying drone cam, in defiance of the rules, sped over her head to photograph Annabel as she was lifted from her rocky prison. Annabel sprawled limp in an engineer's arms, Hannah's mother grabbing for her but restrained by workmen until the doctor could examine the small body for breaks and trauma. Hannah screamed, "Is she alive? *Is she alive?*"

"Yes," somebody said, and caught Hannah as she collapsed into grateful sobs.

Annabel lay unconscious for nearly a month. Her third birthday came and went. Her parents, Hannah, and press from around the world haunted the hospital. MRI, CAT scan, blood tests—all negative. She had not even lost any toes to hypothermia. Her head showed no signs of trauma or concussion under any tests that modern medicine could devise. Her reflexes all looked normal, and her breathing was regular. No one understood.

Then, after four weeks, Annabel opened her eyes, saw her mother, and said, "I fell down."

Hannah, sitting with her mother by Annabel's hospital bed, ripped off the iPod with which she'd been trying to make life bearable, and started to cry. In that moment she vowed she would never yell at anybody again. It was a measure of something—guilt, remorse, love for her little sister—that she kept the vow for almost three whole weeks.

MIRACLE GIRL, the press shrieked.

The surviving organisms began to emerge from their hiding place. Along and inside Annabel's nerves, where the chicken-pox virus could hide for decades before emerging as shingles, the microbes struggled to survive. These alien cells furnished enough chemicals for the microbes to derive energy. The enemy was the soldiers of the host's immune system: cells that engulfed and ate, or exuded deadly toxins, or drilled through the microbes' outer membranes.

The organisms fought back by changing the molecules displayed on their coats, incorporating as much of the host's own tissue as possible in order to fool the immune system and escape detection. They produced chemicals to neutralize toxins. They hid inside cells. The battle was fierce, swift, and expensive, the goals both to survive and to avoid triggering such a massive attack from the immune system that the host died. When the battle was over, only a fraction of the organism remained, its cells too scattered to signal its mates, each alone in a vast alien ecology.

II: October, 2015

"SHE LOOKS FINE, MRS. SEVLEY," the family doctor said. "How old are you now, Annabel?"

"Don't you know?" she said. "You're the doctor!"

"Annabel!" her mother said, but the doctor only laughed.

"Of course I know. I know everything."

Annabel's eyes grew round. "Really? Everything in the whole world?"

"Everything except one thing. Do you like school?"

"I do!" Annabel bounced on the edge of the examining table. "I'm in kindergarten! And I'm five!"

"What's your favorite part of school?"

"Drawing."

"I used to like to draw, too, when I was in kindergarten."

The child looked doubtfully at the old man. "You were in kindergarten?"

"A very long time ago."

"Annabel," Julia Sevley said, "go sit with Hannah in the waiting room. I want to talk to the doctor."

"Okay." She hopped down and ran out.

Julia said, "Everything looks normal? All the blood work?"

"No change at all from six months ago. Why?"

"She has dreams. I don't mean of the accident, she doesn't remember that at all. But she has a lot of nightmares for a five-year-old, a lot more than Hannah did."

"Every child is different, Mrs. Sevley."

"I know. But she wakes whimpering almost every night. And some of her drawings are…disturbing."

"Disturbing how?"

"I don't know. The colors are odd, and they aren't of houses or people or anything. Just pages and pages of odd colors. It seems that, at her age, her pictures should be more detailed and sophisticated. Her best friend, a boy named Keith who's Annabel's age, seems far more advanced."

The old doctor was not a Freudian, a Jungian, or a child psychologist. He dealt mostly in ear infections, broken arms, and stomach flu, with very little patience for the kind of parent who considered their children to be competitors in some sort of developmental marathon. And Mrs. Sevley had always struck him as borderline paranoid. He said, "Her drawing will develop greater sophistication in time. Relax, Mrs. Sevley. Annabel is fine."

Julia tried to look relieved.

In the waiting room Annabel jumped onto a chair beside her sister. Hannah sat staring at nothing. Annabel stood on her chair so she could see the top of Hannah's head. Faint wires, the color of Hannah's glossy black curls and almost invisible, were laced through her hair.

"I know what that thing is and Mom said they're bad! I heard her! She said it to Mrs. Brywood!"

"It's none of your effing business!"

"And Mom said not to swear! I'm telling!"

Hannah snatched off the mesh cap and stuffed it into her pocket. "If you tell Mom, I'll tell her you stole two cookies this morning! I saw you!"

"I don't care," Annabel said stoutly. "Taking cookies isn't as bad as that thing."

"Yes, it is."

"No, it isn't!" They glared at each other, the five-year-old with grubby fingers and the fifteen-year-old who had, all at once, become beautiful. Hannah's eyes, however, were swollen and red under her too-thick black eyeliner. Annabel changed tactics. "If you let me try it on once, I won't tell Mom you have it. *Forever* I won't tell her. I won't tell anybody, not even Keith."

Hannah hesitated. "Well…all right. But only for a minute, and not here."

"Okay!"

"Come on, girls," their mother said, emerging from the doctor's office. "Let's go."

Hannah's bedroom was hung with the new programmed posters of pop stars. Mutely the singers' mouths opened and closed; Hannah had the sound off. Annabel liked better the pictures she herself drew. Those didn't move but they had brighter colors, and these singers wore mostly black and sang against the dull black backgrounds Hannah had chosen. She was into black. However, Annabel said nothing about Hannah's singers in case Hannah changed her mind about this thrilling adventure.

"Han-Han—"

"Don't call me that."

"Hannah, what's this thing called?"

"An N-cap. N for 'neural.'"

"What does it do? Where did it come from? Why doesn't Mom want you to have it?"

"It…how am I going to explain this to a dandelion like you? It comes from Asia, smuggled in on big ships. Mom doesn't want me to have it because she's so reactionary lame. It sends tiny electric signals to your brain that—"

"Electric? Really? Like in the motor of the *car*?"

"No. Yes. These are just tiny little sparks to the part of your brain that makes you feel happier and more energetic. Like when you eat too much sugar."

"Then why don't you just eat sugar?"

"I don't want to get fat," Hannah said. "Besides, it's not exactly like that. It jolts your brain into making more dopamine."

"What is—"

"Never mind! Do you want to try this or not?"

"Yes."

Hannah settled the cap on Annabel's head. "I'm going to keep the controller. See, it's this tiny thing here, and it can go in any body part where I can squeeze the muscles and—"

Annabel giggled. "I know! It can go between the cheeks of your ass! Ava at school told me!"

"Then if you already know all about it, why are you bothering me?"

"I'm sorry! Don't take it off me, Hannah! Make it work!"

Hannah gave a theatrical sigh and closed the fingers of one hand on the controller.

Annabel's mouth opened in a wide pink O. Her eyes opened so wide that their whites dwarfed the irises. She rose onto her tiptoes, her eyes crossed, and she fell onto the floor.

"Annabel! Annabel!"

The child stirred. She looked at Hannah as if at a goddess. "It was…it made me…"

"It's not supposed to make you fall over! Oh, God, are you all right?"

"Yes. It gots…it gots…" Words failed her.

"It's too big a jolt for you! I should have realized, it's not supposed to be for children, you don't have enough body weight—are you sure you're all right?"

"Yes." Annabel rubbed the top of her head.

Curiosity replaced fear. "Did it make you feel happy?"

"I don't know," Annabel said.

"You don't *know*?"

"It gots—"

"It '*has*,'" her sister corrected automatically.

"It gots wrongness," Annabel said.

Hannah snatched the cap off Annabel's head. "You don't know anything. You're just a dandelion."

Annabel ignored this, although ordinarily it would have started another argument. Her eyes had returned to normal. She said, "Hannah, does the N-cap make you happier?"

"Yes."

"Are you not happy 'cause of that boy? Jonathan?"

Hannah blinked. "Sometimes you see more than I think you do."

"Why doesn't Mom want you to be happy in the N-cap?"

"These stronger models can be addictive."

"What's that?"

"Oh, never mind. I'm tired of talking to you, you're such a baby!"

Again Annabel ignored the fighting words. She said slowly, as if working something out in her mind, "The N-cap...I don't like it. When it was on, I wasn't...I wasn't me."

"You don't understand anything, after all," Hannah said dismissively. "You're too young."

A knock on the door. Hannah whisked the N-cap out of sight. Their mother's voice said through the door, "Dinner's ready, girls."

"Is Daddy home?" Annabel called.

Hannah said bitterly, "Of course not. When is he ever? And remember—you promised to never, ever tell Mom!"

For years, the organisms struggled in their new environment. After they were adequately cloaked from the immune system, after they learned how much of the ambient chemicals they could take without harming the host's functioning, had come the long attempt to reconnect. Separated from each other by the vast distances inside the host and by their individual adaptive strategies, they could not trade chemical signals.

But they had been created with many resources, although none that allowed them to take over the genetic machinery of their host cells. The invaders had been intended to evolve and adapt. They developed new internal cellular machinery. Through trial and error, they looked for chemicals that would function with their adapting messaging system. Also through trial and error they learned about their host's cells. And if their efforts sometimes disrupted Annabel's nerve cells and sent strange electrochemical firings to her brain, the disturbances so far were minor. And silent.

"*Now,* Frank?" Mom whimpered. "You want a divorce now, with the economy tanking again and Annabel having strange dreams and these weird—"

"Stop, Julia!" Daddy shouted. He was much louder than Mom. Annabel could hear him through the hallway wall, on her way back from the bathroom. "When would be a good time, tell me that? You see disaster at every day of every year, you always have, and I'm tired of living with someone who's afraid of a crack in the sidewalk and can't make up her mind about anything!"

"You can't just—"

"I can," Daddy said, "and I will."

"It's your new dental hygienist, isn't it, the bimbo who—"

"I'll tell you what," Daddy said, more quietly, "I'll enjoy my new life, and you can enjoy your moral superiority to my new life, and we'll both be happy."

"Annabel," Hannah said, "what are you doing crouching there like that? Are you—oh."

Annabel hadn't heard Hannah, still in her coat and boots, come up behind her, because Daddy was shouting again. Annabel said to Hannah, "Are they going to get a divorce?"

"We can only hope so," Hannah said, scooped up Annabel in her arms, and carried her back to bed. Annabel clung to her big sister. Hannah smelled of shampoo and the cold air from outside and safety. Behind them, Annabel could hear Mom crying, "Don't leave me, Frank, don't just leave us—"

Hannah said, "I will never let a man reduce me to that. Never."

III: September, 2018

HANNAH STOOD SURVEYING HER ROOM, mother, and sister. Tomorrow Hannah was leaving for college in Boston, forty miles away. She had stripped the walls of their art and boxed up all her books, wanting to leave no trace of herself, but the floor looked like an explosion at Macy's: clothes, pillows, electronics, suitcases, small appliances jumbled in piles. Eight-year-old Annabel rooted in the closet, ass outward, like a small burrowing animal.

"Hannah," she called over her shoulder, "Are you taking this old soccer ball? Can I have it?"

"Sure." Hannah held up a pair of jeans. "Mom, these are really irkly."

"Throw them away."

Instead, Hannah handed them to her mother. "No, they're still whole. Will you start a donations bag? And take them to Goodwill after I go?" It was good to keep Mom busy. Since the divorce, she moped around a lot. Look at her now, sitting slumped over on the edge of the bed, fingering the jeans and unable to make a simple decision what to do with them. For years Dad had made all their lives miserable, he did them a favor by leaving, and yet all Mom could do was droop around like limp spaghetti. Pathetic!

Hannah's lip curled in the unforgiving contempt of eighteen.

Annabel backed out of the closet, dust bunnies in her hair, something clutched in her fist, probably a broken necklace or old music cube. Well, let her have it. Hannah was starting a new life, and everything was going to be different.

Mom said, "You'll call me often, right?"

"Sure," Hannah lied.

"It's just that college campuses are getting so weird now, ever since the second economic collapse. The things you see on the Internet…you'll be careful, Hannah?"

"Sure."

Annabel said, "Can I go over to Keith's?"

Mom said hopelessly, "But this is Hannah's last night, Annie, and I thought we would—"

"Oh, let her go," Hannah said, and Annabel left. Really, her mother was so wimpy. Since the divorce, more and more often it was Hannah who made the decisions. She resented it, and liked it, and tomorrow she would be gone and her mother would just have to take charge again.

Wouldn't she?

Annabel charged through the back door of the Brywoods' house, next door to hers in the eighty-year-old housing development and identical to it, without knocking. Keith's father looked up from a laptop on the kitchen table, said mildly, "Hi, Annabel," and went back to the laptop. Annabel waved at him and ran upstairs to Keith's tiny bedroom.

Keith was her best friend. Becca, her ex-best-friend, said that it was slutty to hang out so much with a boy. Annabel didn't know what "slutty" meant but it didn't sound good, so she punched Becca in the stomach and went back to playing with Keith.

He was really smart. Like her, he was in the third grade, but he knew the names of fifteen different snakes, how to get to Level 8 in Smash You!, who invented sandwiches, and why demons were waking up right now and not, say, ten years ago.

Annabel was sorry the demons hadn't stayed safely asleep until she was grown up, but it was just one of those things. Keith liked blue light and had ordered a whole lot of blue light bulbs over the Internet. His room was always bathed in a cool shade of blue that made everyone look like zombies or aliens.

"Keith! Look what I got! I took it from Hannah's closet—a underground cube about angels!"

Keith looked up from his computer. "So?"

"So we can watch it! It's *underground.*"

Keith gazed at her. He could be snotty sometimes, because he was so smart. Annabel often wished she was as smart as Keith, or Hannah. Or maybe as pretty as Mom. Or as sure of himself as Dad, who she saw once every few months. Dad always got what he wanted.

Keith was short and round, and in his black-and-white tee he looked a lot like the soccer ball that Hannah had just given Annabel. Maybe she should have brought that, instead of the underground cube, since Keith didn't seem very impressed. But then her native stubbornness kicked in and she put her hand on her hip. "Well, *I'm* going to watch it! Close that program!"

Keith did, following their usual pattern: Annabel proposed, he objected, she overruled him and he gave in with a sigh that said he was only going along with this to be nice. Annabel dragged a second chair up to Keith's desk and they loaded the cube. That the program was even on a cube made it exciting; the clumsy manual loading overrode the parental controls installed by Keith's mother.

The angel program, however, was disappointing. It started out well enough, with a spooky voice saying from drifting clouds: "Not only demons are waking on Earth—angels are returning to us as well! The apocalypse approaches!" The clouds got all thundery and lightning flashed. Annabel shivered deliciously and put her hand on Keith's arm. But after that the cube turned out to be just a bunch of people talking about prophecies and end times. No wonder Hannah had thrown it into the back of her closet.

Keith closed it down before it was over. "They should have had angels and demons fighting. With swords and lightning bolts and magic and stuff. But I got something better than that."

"Yeah? What?" Annabel was now down one, and skepticism was called for in order to even the scales.

"This!" Keith wriggled under the bed and came up with a glittery mesh net.

Instantly Annabel recoiled. "No!"

He stared at her. "What's wrong with you? It's an N-cap!"

"I know what it is!"

"You do? How?"

"I tried one once. Hannah's. It's…it's nasty."

"Well, I never tried it, and I'm going to. It's a new kind, and really strong. That's what my cousin David said. I was saving it for us to do together, Annie!"

"Where did you get it?"

"I stole it from David." Keith had a huge number of cousins, mostly male, a few of whom were in jail. Annabel's mother was unaware of this. She let Annabel go over to Keith's so often because she liked his parents, sweet-natured and quiet people who took walks together and held hands when they watched TV, which was another reason Annabel liked being at the Brywood house.

She said, "I don't want to do any N-cap. It's a bad thing."

"Bad how?"

Annabel shook her head, her face mutinous, but said nothing. Keith rolled his eyes at her and put the cap on his head. The silvery mesh changed color to match his dark curls. The tiny controller hung from the cap by a fine string, which Keith had neglected to remove. It fell across his nose, tickling him into a sneeze. He blew the string to the side—whuff!— and pressed the controller button.

Annabel watched closely. Her stomach roiled, although she had no idea why.

Keith's mouth opened wide. His eyes crossed, uncrossed, and then unfocused. His lips curved upward in pure joy. As soon as the jolt of electricity to the pleasure center in his brain faded, he pressed the button again. And then again.

Annabel tore the mesh net off his head. The string holding it to the remote snapped.

"Give that to me!" Keith yelled.

"No! It's bad!"

Keith lunged for her. Annabel, taller and with long skinny legs like a crane, was faster. She was out the door and running down the stairs before Keith could grab the N-cap.

"Give it to me!"

Annabel flew through the kitchen, bumping the table. "Hey!" Mr. Brywood said. "Play tag somewhere else!" By the time Keith caught up to her, she'd shoved the N-cap down the city trash compactor at the end of the street, one of the few that still worked. The compactor made its grinding noise.

Keith screamed, "You had no right to do that! It was mine!"

"It was bad!"

Keith hit her, not very effectively. She hit him back, with stronger results. They both went home and didn't speak to each other for a week.

"*Bad*," Annabel murmured to herself. Everything was bad: Hannah going away, and the stupid angel cube, and the N-cap, and the whole world. A few demons and angels and witches and fighting would greatly improve things. At least it would be more interesting.

The microbes were more secure. Through evolution, adaptation, and sheer luck, they had found a way to attach themselves to nerve cell membranes, along with various receptors and transport mechanisms. Microtubules connected them to the cell's cytoplasm. From this vantage point they seemed enough a part of the cell to not attract the attention of the immune system. But they still had to evolve chemical signals that would let them communicate with each other in this strange tissue. Signaling would enable them to once again become not individual organisms but a complex and working whole.

The microbes had time. Annabel's body, nerves, brain were still growing, still very plastic. Her neural network was a long way from maturity. The way her brain handled information yielded to even massive modification.

"This is the Age of Imagination," the professor said from the front of the class. "The previous three hundred years, from the middle of the eighteenth century on, was the Age of Science. Now the balance is being righted; the other half of the human mind is being given its rightful place; the old rationalism is being shown to be—not wrong, because obviously there is a place for science—but limited. Unbalanced when taken alone. Insufficient to encompass the incredible variety of the universe."

Hannah spoke into her wrister, "Age of Imagination, science true but insufficient, other half of human mind." The lecture was being recorded on her tablet, of course, but she had developed her own method of oral note-taking, keyed to tablet locations. The course, "Introduction to Domains of Experience," was a prerequisite for all history courses, and nearly six hundred students sat in the ancient lecture hall, wood-paneled in rising tiers of old-fashioned tables. There wouldn't be much opportunity to ask questions.

"Consider," said the professor, young and energetic, "the basic tenet of science: that experiments be replicable. That automatically cuts from consideration hosts of phenomena that have been documented but are singular. Did miracles ever occur on Earth? Sightings of ghosts? Angelic visitations? Demon possession? The satori claimed by meditating monks? Whatever happened to Saul on the road to Damascus? Clairvoyant dreams? Feelings of déjà vu? For centuries people have claimed to experience these things, and science has said, 'No, you didn't experience it because it cannot be replicated.' Were all those people mistaken? Lying? Deluded? All of them? Is faith itself nothing but a delusion?"

Hannah lowered her wrister, frowning.

"I ask you to consider another possibility," the professor said. "Consider this: that there are different domains of experience available to the human mind. Science is one, and certainly valid. However, it is—in mathematical terms—necessary but insufficient. Consider that humanity has stunted itself by declaring a different kind of experience inferior. Consider that most people who are not scientists or intellectuals have not been misled by this narrowness but have gone on holding to the domain of faith. Consider that faith does not have to be religious, but rather that religion may be a subset of faith: faith that the universe contains more phenomena than we have yet explained, or that we can explain. That the phenomena which for thousands of years people have claimed to experience—demons, angels, witches, magic—all pejorative terms in the canon of science—may actually all be *real*. Only now are these things being acknowledged as a legitimate area of human study. Now, in the Age of Imagination."

Hannah bit her lip. He was charismatic, but more than that, what he was saying made sense. And wasn't there something her mother had once said about some older cousin of hers, Paula Somebody, who'd written letters about something weird someplace in South America....And yet, something here wasn't right.

None of the students around her seemed to share her misgivings. They were nodding, smiling. A few looked thoughtful, a few downright eager.

Hannah raised her hand. Among the six hundred students, he saw her—maybe, Hannah thought cynically but accurately, because she was pretty. He said, "Yes?"

"Do *you* believe those supernatural things are real?"

"Do you?" he said, with what was probably supposed to be twinkling charm. Hannah didn't charm that easily. She saw the answer in his face: Yes, he believed.

She said, "Isn't there another explanation for the rise of the Age of Imagination? In times of great uncertainty, people turn to whatever comfort they can find. We have all these drug-resistant infections that no antibiotics can do anything about and so people lost faith in doctors. A few years ago we had the second economic collapse in this century when China lost its markets in Japan and Europe buckled under debt and—"

Classmates around her were tittering.

The professor said, smiling, "Those are exactly the objections the rigid, hide-bound 'rationalists' make. Anything to avoid seeing what's directly under their noses, and has been for centuries."

"But—"

"There are no 'buts' to this. We are in a new, dynamic age of expanded perceptions."

"Or of wish-fulfillment delusions."

A boy in a tier behind her booed. Two girls in front of Hannah turned to sneer. The professor went on smiling, with gentle pity. Hannah picked up her tablet and walked out.

Halloween. Hannah planned on staying in and studying.

"Oh, come on out with us!" her roommate Jenna said. "It's going to be so much fun!"

"Can't. I have an exam Monday in Political Theory."

"I can tell you all about political theory in one sentence. The theory is that the world's politics are fucked. Now come with me and Ava to the party."

Hannah looked up at her roomie. Jenna was hard to resist—warm, sparkly. Hannah knew she was not sparkly, was sometimes even dour. If she hadn't been so pretty, she might have had a very bad time at college, despite her brains. But she was pretty, and eighteen, and it was Halloween, and Jenna was right about one thing: the political economy was fucked. Unemployment had reached twenty-eight percent, federal debt outpaced her—or anybody else's—generation's ability to pay it off, and economic growth was stagnant. There might not be very many parties in anybody's future. If it hadn't been for the great divorce settlement Mom had gotten, Hannah might not be in college at all. And Julia had only gotten that settlement because Hannah had insisted on a tough lawyer. If it had been left up to Mom—or to Hannah's bastard father—she and Hannah and Annabel would be living in a cardboard box.

"Okay," she said to Jenna, " I'll come. Do I have to have a costume? And what is that you're almost wearing?"

Jenna's brief halter and see-though skirt were Day-Glo yellow, topped by a pair of wings that kept falling off her shoulders. "I'm a fairy. See—here's my wand." She flourished a dowel topped by a tin-foil star.

"You're going to be a really cold fairy. It's *October*."

"I can manage. What can we make you for a costume? Here's Hannah, the great planner, without a costume! Let me see, we can—"

"I'll just be a ghost," Hannah said, grabbing the sheet off her bed.

"No!" All at once Jenna stood rigid and serious.

Hannah stared at her in astonishment. "What's with you?"

"You can't be a ghost. This is a party, Hannah—a *party*. I don't want to risk an inadvertent summoning."

So there they were again, at that same place. Hannah tried hard to avoid that place because she liked Jenna. Jenna was sweet-natured, generous, and a believer in the supernatural all the way. In her, the Age of Imagination had become the Age of Irrationality. And there were so many Jennas on campus.

Hannah said, "Maybe I won't go, after all."

"You're going, and you're going now, and you're going in costume. Here, what about this?" Jenna pulled a coat of green, very shaggy wool from her own closet.

"A coat? What am I supposed to be—a store mannequin?"

"No, you're a yard! It'll be great! We put some paper flowers on you and a picket fence on your head…" She was folding pink tissues and tossing Hannah scissors and white cardboard. When they were done and Hannah looked at herself in the mirror, she had to laugh. And certainly nobody else would come to the party as a yard.

Nor a ghost, witch, demon, or angel. Hannah was surprised to even see a girl dressed as a black cat. But despite the silly superstitions, she enjoyed the party, until about eleven. Then, as everybody started to seem drunk, Hannah, a non-drinker, left. She could still get in a few hours of study.

Halfway back to her dorm, cardboard fence and tissue flowers no longer on her head, she crossed a parking lot. A half dozen masked people dragged a boy, screaming, toward a dilapidated vehicle shed.

Hannah raised her wrister to call Security. Before she could speak, one of the draggers sprinted to her, knocked down her arm, and tore off the wrister.

Hannah's breath tangled in her throat. What would they do to her, to the boy? He had stopped screaming. The masked boy gripping her arm said, "You're going to stand here quietly with me and then you're going to go back to your dorm or apartment or wherever you snobs live. This doesn't concern you."

On his costume, some sort of antiquated soldier with a full face mask, she saw a homemade badge with red letters: SLA.

"Let me go!"

He did, but he kept her wrister, and he stood close enough to keep her from bolting. Two of the girls with the group kicked in the flimsy shed door.

Hannah forced words up her tightening throat. "What did he do?"

The boy said, "He put a curse on my friend."

Clearly, he believed it. This townie and the college kid had gotten into some sort of argument or fight—it happened all the time, usually when everyone was drunk—and the dragged boy had shouted something childish like "You're screwed, man!" Then the other guy had fallen ill, or lost his job, or whatever. This boy and his band of whackos genuinely believed his friend had been cursed, because the domain of non-replicable experience was just as real as science. Not that he would ever phrase it like that.

Her captor said, "Don't move until I let you."

"I won't," Hannah said, and kicked him in the balls.

He went down silently, which surprised her, clutching his crotch. She grabbed her wrister from his hand and took a precious moment to snatch the mask from his face and memorize him. Then she was running, knowing that none of them could catch her; she'd lettered in track. As soon as she reached a lighted area with other people, she phoned the cops.

A curse. And they all believed it. Why not? On this campus there were courses examining the documented evidence of Dobu Islanders who died because they believed they were cursed, of Americans relieved of pain because they believed their placebos were real, of cancer victims with a higher survival rate than control groups because others prayed for them. Belief was a powerful thing.

And, she hadn't really grasped before, a dangerous one.

Hannah went down to the precinct and identified the boy she'd kicked in the groin, who was charged with assault. He didn't give up his confederates and they were never caught. A cop told her the crude SLA patch meant Supranatural Liberation Army, a loose collective of believers in the paranormal that had started on the Internet and was growing exponentially across the nation. "Psychos, the worst of them. The FBI is finally getting interested."

Just before Thanksgiving, Hannah was surprised when her Domains of Experience professor sat next to her in the cafeteria. "Hello, Hannah. May I talk to you?"

"Sure." She closed her new tablet. Up close, Dr. Paluski smelled of some spicy aftershave that was disturbing.

"I want to know why, after such excellent initial work, you've stopped coming to my class."

Jenna was staring at them, open-mouthed, from a nearby table. Hannah blurted, "It's dangerous."

He smiled, and she realized she'd said the wrong thing. He said, "Challenging old beliefs, widening one's mental horizons—those things are always dangerous."

"That's not what I meant." He was still smiling, which both angered her and, obscurely, forced her to continue. "People twist the doctrine of different domains. They use it to justify all sorts of irrationality, even violent ones."

His smile vanished but his patronizing tone didn't. "But, Hannah, that's true of science as well. Both modes of experience are just tools. When cavemen discovered fire, the crime of arson became possible. Knowing the structure of the atom led to nuclear weapons, and decoding the human genome to the kind of biological weapons that wiped out so much of Pakistan. Similarly, imagination can be used for evil or for reaching truths not available to science. So—"

Something snapped in her. "Truths, Dr. Paluski? Really? Look at this poll from today's news." She opened her tablet and the news avatars sprang into three-dimensional holo life off its surface. Hannah put their caperings, as well as the charts and graphs and illustrations that changed ceaselessly behind them, on mute. She said, "Seventy-seven percent of Americans believe there is a war going on between angels and demons and that both sides are now actively recruiting or possessing humans to fight it. Forty-three percent believe they have personally been contacted in this war. Fifty-two percent believe they know someone who has been cursed or has put an effective curse on someone else. Twenty-six percent believe levitation is possible, thirty-one percent that aliens directed evolution, another forty-two percent that evolution never happened, and fully eighty-two percent that ghosts regularly affect the affairs of the living. Eighty—"

"Hannah, Hannah, this is all part of a transition to a wider world view. You're studying history—how much turmoil attended the switch in the eighteenth century from the Age of Faith to the Enlightenment?"

"Turmoil? You want turmoil?" Her voice had risen and students were turning from their tablets and wristers to look at her. "I'll give you turmoil! Yesterday in Dallas a girl died during an exorcism. Two days ago a group of mothers in suburban Philadelphia—suburban mothers!—attacked a homeless man because they believed he was cursing their children. This morning the CDC released their weekly Morbidity and Mortality Report and they've added a new category to their list: 'Nocebo-Caused Illness/Death.' That means the causation of sickness or death purely by expecting it. Last week's figure was higher than for influenza."

He said, "You're a very smart girl, Hannah. But I repeat: the Enlightenment caused all kinds of turmoil, too. For instance, the American Revolution."

"We don't need another one."

"Don't stop attending my course. It's required and you'll wreck a potentially outstanding GPA."

"I don't care," she said, just as Jenna came up to them.

"Hi, Hannah. You're Dr. Paluski, aren't you?" she cooed. "I really wish I'd been in your section of Domains of Experience. Hannah said that you're just the most charismatic teacher ever."

Hannah laughed.

The boy who had grabbed Hannah came to trial, and she testified. The only evidence of her being assaulted was a faint bruise on one arm, photographed that night by the cops, but the prosecutor had something else in mind. He used the half-century-old RICO, Racketeer Influenced and Corrupt Organizations Act, to argue that the gang which attacked the college student was a "criminal enterprise," and therefore Hannah's attacker could be held responsible for the boy's beating, too. Hannah, sitting on a hard, battered pew in the ancient courthouse, was enthralled. The prosecutor's argument marched along in clean, straight lines. So did the defense attorney's, although not as strongly.

The boy, glaring at Hannah as he was led in cuffs from the courtroom, was convicted. Hannah had a sudden insight: Law was the only restraint against the abuses caused by a culture unrestrained by rationality. Science could not restrain the current madness—hadn't some important scientist said once that "When culture and science clash, science always loses"?

Too esoteric, specialized, and difficult, battered by recent economic and epidemiological events, science was losing now.

She was going to become a lawyer.

Three days later she went home for Christmas break, to find Annabel too thin and their mother drunk.

Annabel watched anxiously from the front door as the taxi pulled into the driveway and Hannah got out with her suitcase. "I'm glad you're here," Annabel said in a small voice after Hannah had come inside on a swoosh of cold air. "Maybe we can put up the Christmas tree?"

She didn't really want the Christmas tree. She only wanted things to go back to the way they'd been, before they got so awful. She hadn't told Hannah how awful, not once during all the long time she was away, because Mom had said not to: Hannah was very busy studying and they shouldn't worry her.

"Where's Mom?" Hannah said. She sniffed at the front hall, which smelled of vomit even though Annabel had tried to scrub it out of the rug.

"Upstairs," Annabel said.

"And she can't come down to greet me?"

"She's asleep."

Hannah took the stairs two at a time. Annabel raced after her, her belly churning. Maybe Mom wouldn't be....

Mom was.

Hannah looked around the room, filthy and malodorous, an empty bottle fallen from her mother's slack hand. When Hannah shook her, Mom didn't wake. Hannah turned to look at Annabel. Hannah was going to blame her! She should have taken better care of her mother, she should have—Annabel burst into tears.

Hannah picked her up and carried her into her own room, untouched since she'd left for college. "Tell me, Annie," she said gently. "Tell me everything."

"Mom drinks that bad stuff," Annabel sobbed, "and Keith—" But she couldn't tell about Keith. He'd get in trouble. "And I have bad dreams!"

"Of course you do," Hannah soothed. "Anybody would, living like this. But it's going to be all right now. I promise."

"Are you going to call Daddy?"

"Daddy? No." Hannah's lips tightened. "But it's going to be all right. I promise, Annabel."

Hannah took all the bad bottles out of the house. She shouted at their mother. She put up the Christmas tree, and on Christmas morning there were presents. She made a lot of phone calls. Another taxi came and took Mom "to a hospital for a month, where she can get better." Hannah was there for three weeks of the month, and then Aunt Judy came to stay for a while and take care of Annabel. When Mom came home, she was quiet and didn't say much and went to a lot of meetings, but she didn't drink anymore. Hannah had fixed everything.

Except Keith, and the dreams.

The organisms' first attempts at chemical signaling to each other were both slow and disastrous. The right chemicals were not available, and new ones had to be tried, discarded, tried again. Mindless trial-and-error, for without communication, the microbes were not yet a unified mind. Sometimes their attempts killed host cells. Sometimes they mobilized T-cells. Sometimes they triggered inadvertent firings of a neural network that bombarded Annabel's brain stem as she slept.

Then she dreamed, incoherently and too much.

IV: May, 2024

ANNABEL AND HER MOTHER were going to take the train to Boston for Hannah's graduation from Harvard Law. Mom had at first been hesitant because of the SLA flash mobs that often turned into riots, but Annabel had insisted. "I'm not going to miss this, and there's no other way to get there!"

"But if those people block the train, or the T…"

Mom had become so hesitant, so fearful. She wasn't drinking anymore, but she seldom left the house and seemed unable to make the smallest decisions. Annabel was more compassionate than Hannah. She said soothingly, "They won't block the trains," although of course they might. The SLA, which had grown in numbers as the depression ground on and on and mini-epidemics broke out in more and more cities, could decide that a train was cursed, or haunted, or just necessary to their war efforts. The war against the demons went well some days, not so well others, depending on—what? Annabel didn't know, and didn't greatly care. She'd grown up with the war. It was just there, like air, and like air quality, you coped with it and stayed inside when it got too bad. Law enforcement also tried to cope with it, but there were so many members of the SLA, and, linked by elaborate cell phone networks, they could appear and disappear like smoke.

None of that was going to stop Annabel. She was going to Hannah's graduation. Not because her father would be there; she'd long ago lost the desire to have a relationship with him or his new wife. No, she was going because it was Hannah, the person Annabel loved most in the world. Annabel would have given anything to be more like Hannah. Hannah had finished her B.A. in three years, been on the *Harvard Law Review*, graduated ninth in her class. Since Annabel wasn't ever going to be as brilliant or energetic as Hannah, she pawned her grandmother's wedding ring—at fourteen, she was getting good at pawning things—and bought two train tickets.

The night before the trip to Boston, she steeled herself and went next door to see Keith.

His mother had died six months ago during an eruption of drug-resistant meningitis. Mr. Brywood had just fallen apart. The death had been a grief to Keith, too, but also an excuse. Annabel braced herself for the coming argument. If he was wearing that thing…

He wasn't. Dressed in a loose bathrobe, he sat with his tablet but blanked it so fast when she opened the bedroom door that he'd probably been looking at porn. Well, porn was a step up. The blue light bulbs he still liked colored everything with eerie shadows. "Hey, Keith."

"Hey, Annabel."

"We're going to Boston tomorrow for Hannah's graduation and I wanted to say good-bye."

"Hannah's graduating? Already?"

She'd told him several times about the graduation, the trip, all of it. Anger started somewhere deep in her belly, a seed starting to push upward. "Have you been doing it?"

"No."

Had he always been such a poor liar? "Give it to me."

"Not a chance in hell."

"Don't say that!" Annabel blurted.

He jeered, "What, you afraid of a summoning?"

She wasn't, exactly. After all, she'd never actually seen the things that the SLA said could be summoned from hell: demons, ghosts, succubi, witches, loa, serpents that dissolved into a person and cursed them. But of course, that didn't mean they didn't exist. She'd never seen a black hole, either, or a virus. She said, "Where is it, Keith?"

"I don't know what you're talking about."

She might have believed him. His eyes were clear, he'd been looking at normal porn, and Hannah's graduation might have just slipped his mind. But then an odor wafted toward her, and she flung open the closet door. It was all there: uneaten sandwiches, uneaten tacos, uneaten pizza, all crawling with bugs. Keith had smuggled the meals upstairs, or made his father bring them up here, and then consumed none of them.

"You *are* doing it! Where is it?"

"I told you—"

Frenzy seized her. She began to tear open drawers on the dresser—but no, he'd have it closer to him. She barreled into Keith and easily knocked him off his chair. Underneath the voluminous bathrobe he was just a sack of bones. He'd been sitting on the N-cap. It was the newest Chinese model, illegal in every state of the union, capable of stimulating the pleasure center of the brain every few seconds until the wearer, ecstatic, starved to death, laughing with joy.

Keith bawled, "Give that to me!"

Annabel sprinted for the door, but desperation drove Keith and he was bigger and faster than he had been six years ago. He grabbed her ankles and pulled her down. In a moment he had the N-cap away from her. Annabel, recognizing that even in his weakened state he was taller and stronger, didn't try to get it back. Tears sprang into her eyes.

"Keith, you're going to kill yourself."

"You don't know what you're talking about."

"Yes! I do!"

"I think you should go," he said. His fingers played restlessly over the mesh cap. He couldn't wait to put it back on.

Annabel stood. Reaching over to his tablet, she unblanked it. He hadn't been watching porn, after all. He didn't need porn. The Internet played a homework assignment from three weeks ago, a cover in case his father came upstairs. Annabel recognized it from history class. Keith had spoken none of the answers into the three-dimensional structure connecting historical events. The smartest boy in their year, he was failing every class.

Tell Mr. Brywood? It wouldn't help. He was destroyed by grief, he couldn't watch Keith twenty-four hours a day, and there were no treatment centers left for the "differently imaginative." None that the Brywood family could afford.

"I'm not going to watch you die," she said to Keith. "I'm never coming back here."

He didn't answer, merely fingered the mesh cap hungrily. As Annabel closed the door, he was already fitting it onto his head.

Annabel's mother didn't go to Hannah's graduation, after all. The morning news avatars reported a massive rally on Boston Commons. The Massachusetts Federation of Witches and Warlocks were defying the SLA, hoping to convince viewers that their own arts were white magic, not allied with demons. Men, women, and children, many wearing pentacle jewelry, sang and chanted peacefully. Boston PD in riot gear stood at the edges of the crowd and around the speaker's dais, their crowd-dispersing sound machines beside them. But when the drone cams zoomed in on the cops' faces, many looked sympathetically at the witches and warlocks. Just as many, however, had the hard-jawed look of people more than ready to attack.

"We can't go," Mom said. "It's too dangerous. Hannah will understand."

Annabel heard the relief in her mother's voice, and said nothing.

Her mother said defensively, "Hannah will understand. Annabel, did I ever tell you about my older cousin Paula, who actually encountered a demon in the jungles of Nicaragua?"

"Yes, Mom. You did." When her mother went into the bathroom, Annabel took her suitcase and train ticket and walked the mile to the station.

The train was late. As she waited on the platform, a sagging wood-and-concrete structure that there was no municipal money to maintain, a woman walked by wheeling a baby carriage, and something happened to Annabel's entire body. She froze. Then a deep shudder ran from her legs clear upward to the back of her neck. For a long moment she couldn't move, not a muscle. Then the spasm was over and Annabel abruptly sank down to the platform.

"Miss, are you all right?" a man said.

"I…y…yes." It was difficult to speak. What had just happened to her?

The man helped her to her feet. The train sped around a curve of track. Annabel's spasm passed, and she got on the train for Boston.

Seven more years, and the organisms, now all throughout Annabel's sympathetic and parasympathetic nervous systems, had mastered signaling to each other. Slowly a complex second network was evolving inside Annabel, a second ecosystem, using the chemicals and proteins already in her body, and made possible by the very rapid life cycle of the organism's individual units. The components of the network had their own differentiated functions.

The entity had vastly increased its ability to learn about the host's functions. Already it could intercept and interpret molecules coming from outside the host to its olfactory system.

A new smell came to the entity. New, and old. The microbial network was electrified, literally. Chemical signaling prompted nerve firings. Another host! It smelled just like the current host, it was fresh and plastic and….it was gone.

Until the mother wheeled the baby carriage out of range, Annabel stood frozen, the microseizure in her limbic system paralyzing her motor control. Then the seizure ended.

But the evolving entity, smaller than the hundred trillion synaptic connections of Annabel's original brain but growing daily in both size and complexity, remembered.

Just before Framingham, the train jerked to a halt.

Passengers looked at each other, then craned their necks alongside the windows. There was nothing to see except abandoned buildings, farm fields, and an apple orchard in spring bloom. "Get off," a woman said urgently to her husband. "There's going to be trouble." They grabbed their things and hurried to the door, where the husband pressed the emergency button. Alarms sounded.

Annabel clutched her purse, uncertain what to do. A half dozen people were already calling the police on their wristers. She looked again through the window. The escaping couple had reached the apple orchard.

"Nobody move!" Three figures burst in from the next car, all holding guns.

A man across the aisle from Annabel dropped to below the seat back in front of him, drew his own gun, and fired at the invaders. People screamed and one of the figures went down. A moment later the shooter exploded in a fountain of blood.

"I said don't move!" one of the remaining invaders, a woman, said. Her voice held righteous fury. "Any more demons on this train, and we'll know it!"

Annabel sat rigidly in her seat. The man who'd been shot first rose to his feet; he wore some kind of thin, impenetrable body armor under his jacket. The jackets of all three bore the same SLA symbol Annabel had seen just a few hours ago on the news: a confusion of angel wings on a sort of Buddha surrounded by a serpent.

The SLA soldier held an automatic weapon on the car, while the other two moved down the aisle, their own weapons drawn, scrutinizing each face. Did they think they could tell which were demons just by looking? Evidently they could. When they came to Annabel, one put his hand under her chin and raised her eyes to his. She saw that he was only a few years older than she was, and younger than Hannah. The boy's eyes were deep blue, and something in their depths was frightening. Annabel felt warmth surge through her face, then recede, and hated herself for blushing. Something her father used to say when she was very small popped into her mind: *The eyes are the window of the soul.* But whatever the boy saw in Annabel's eyes, he released her chin and passed on.

No one else in the car was a demon.

They were all ordered off the train, which then started up again and disappeared. Standing beside the tracks, her suitcase in one hand and purse in the other, Annabel heard a man say, "They took the train for the war effort. To pick up more soldiers between here and Boston for the battle on the Commons. This could be the big one." His voice held satisfaction.

Annabel had no idea how far they still were from Boston. Could she walk along the track until she got there? Would she be in time for Hannah's graduation?

Other people had started to walk. Annabel, rolling her little suitcase over the rough gravel and weeds, followed them. Three miles later, buses sent by the United States Army picked them all up and took them to a high school being used as a temporary shelter. Boston was under quarantine until the violence could be brought under control. Nobody in, nobody out.

Control didn't take long. The SLA, equipped with Uzis and fanaticism, were nonetheless no match for the army. By evening, the Battle of Boston Commons was over. Nearly six hundred were dead: witches, warlocks, mystics, SLA "soldiers," BPD cops, Hare Krishna, angels and demons and onlookers. Boston remained in quarantine for another two days, until all the dead had been identified. Mr. Brywood drove to the shelter and brought Annabel home. Hannah never did get a graduation ceremony.

***

"Now they have martyrs," Hannah said to Annabel. Her sister's taut, beautiful face—more beautiful than Annabel would ever be—was so clear on the 3-D Internet connection that she seemed to be in Annabel's bedroom. "Both sides have martyrs. The entire nation will end up even more polarized than before, and more lunatic."

Annabel nodded. She sat on the edge of her bed, wrapped in her winter bathrobe and a blanket, even though it was May.

"Annie, are you okay?"

"Yes. Just cold. I think I caught a bug or something on the train."

"Well, take care of yourself. Hydrate. God, when I think of you caught in that insane event…" Hannah smacked her fist on something that Annabel couldn't see, then changed her tone. "How's Mom?"

"She's fine."

"You always were a poor liar. She's hiding out and weeping, isn't she? Filled with guilt over not being with you on the train, which is a great excuse to keep herself immobilized."

Annabel said nothing. She felt so *cold*.

"Annabel, listen to me. You know I start as a junior D.A. tomorrow. I want to use the full power of the law to prosecute these nutjobs. I also want you to come live with me. I have a little apartment in a safe neighborhood—well, as safe as anything is now—and you could finish school here. You shouldn't bury yourself in that geriatric cul-de-sac. Now don't tell me you can't leave Mom. If you're not there to baby her, she'll *have* to take care of herself. This is what is best for everybody. If you'll come, I'll bring you here myself."

Annabel opened her mouth to say no. She knew, without words, that Hannah believed what she was saying, but also that it wasn't the whole truth. Forces worked in Hannah that went beyond reason: her protectiveness of Annabel, her resentment of her mother's weaknesses, her need to be in control. And in Annabel herself, she already knew at fourteen, was a lack of fire, a driftiness reminiscent of her mother, that could all too easily let Hannah dictate the rest of her life. Annabel was not a combative person; in any daily conflict with Hannah, she would lose. She opened her mouth to say no.

Then something happened, which was and wasn't the same something that had happened at the train station. Her body froze for a long moment. Then it was restored to her and it was all she could do to remain sitting upright on the edge of the bed. But this time an image filled her mind, dream-like and surreal, but also so sharp it seemed she could smell it. *Babies.*

The image vanished.

"Yes," she told Hannah. "I'll come."

V: July, 2027

PAUL APLEY SAT in his tiny, cramped office in Cambridge and frowned at the data displayed on his laptop.

The office wasn't actually his. It was an unused storeroom on the MIT campus, on loan to the CDC along with the use of any labs Paul might need. Paul knew that the Dean hoped no labs would be required; college resources were tight enough already, now that so many science buildings had been shut down and so much of the university budget went to Security. But Paul doubted he would need an on-site lab. Neither a field epidemiologist, those wild adventurers, nor a lab man, he worked in data, not gene sequencers.

Something odd had shown up in the weekly data for Boston/Cambridge.

The CDC was extremely sensitive to oddities in data. The big fear, of course, was an epidemic, either natural or bio-engineered. With half the country convinced that it could fight infection through exorcism, prayer, spells, or miracles, the United States was vulnerable. Funding for public health had dropped precipitously as the new culture elected more and more anti-science law-makers. China, the Arab world, and Europe were watching. Global warming, although proceeding much more slowly than originally feared, was still bringing tropical diseases farther and farther north. There was dengue fever in New York City.

However, Paul wasn't looking at a tropical disease, or a plague, or a bio-weapon. He was looking at data on babies.

Infant mortality had dropped in the US, as midwives and home births increasingly replaced deliveries in the microbe-prone and drug-resistant environment of hospitals. But it was not childbirth data that Paul was concerned with.

In the last year, twenty-three children in Boston had been taken to area hospitals after falling into unexplained comas. All were under two years old. Twenty-one of them had had no previous health issues. In each case, doctors had been able to find no cause for the coma. In each case, the infants had spontaneously emerged from coma in three to five weeks. CAT scans, MRIs, and blood work had all come back negative for any known pathogen. Spinal fluid taps had turned up some odd proteins, but as far as could be determined, no identifiable pathogens.

A new and terrible bioweapon?

Toxins from environmental pollution?

A mutated meningitis?

Something hiding in tissues where only an autopsy could identify it, as malaria hid in the human liver during part of its life cycle?

Like most CDC non-field epidemiologists, Paul was focused, orderly, still. Carefully he examined the hospital data available on each child—address, age, weight, ethnicity, medical history—looking for patterns. He didn't expect to find them in this meager supply of information, but knowing what he already had would lead him to what to investigate next. Each of these parents would need to be interviewed. They lived in different areas of the city, worked at different jobs, professed different religions, came from different ethnic backgrounds. Each of these babies was enmeshed in a complex network of relatives, friends, neighbors, caretakers, bus drivers, pets, cleaning products, doctors, and dozens of other factors. But somewhere there was a common thread. He just hoped it wasn't some nutcase voodoo, or cult practice, or brewed-at-home tea guaranteed to bring up memories of past lives. With any luck, none of these parents would have seen the Virgin Mary in a toaster pastry. With any luck.

Annabel put the flimsie down next to her coffee cup and sighed. She would never, ever be able to write like Hannah. Even if she'd stayed in school, which she'd never been outstanding at, she wouldn't have been able to write like that.

Not that she was jealous of Hannah—she wasn't. Her sister struck Annabel as completely admirable, but also a little crazy. The hours she worked! She never relaxed, never stopped to gaze for ten minutes at a sunset, never read a novel, never laughed out loud at a comedian on the Internet. Annabel, who did all these things plus talk to everyone in the neighborhood, felt no envy of Hannah. Also, Annabel loved her job. Jobs, actually, since they kept moving as Hannah's dizzying successes at work brought her more promotions, more high-profile cases, even a little more money when most government salaries were frozen. Now, three years after the Battle of Boston Commons, Hannah was litigating against the SLA appeal of their convictions under the RICO statutes.

And she found time to write for news sites!

Sitting at the kitchen table in their modest apartment, her coffee cooling, Annabel read again Hannah's guest editorial for the *Boston Globe*, which she'd printed onto the flimsie:

SCIENCE, CULTURE, AND MONEY
by Hannah Sevley

Walk down any street in Boston in this hot July and everything looks normal for whatever neighborhood you're in: women watering lawns, men carrying home canvas sacks from the grocery store, children running in and out of the spray from an opened fire hydrant, holo-ads springing up from the sidewalk, homeless relocating yet another tent city in yet another temporary park. And in another sense, our current cultural situation is also normal.

A definition of normal: "In accordance with behavioral norms."

Here are two human behavioral norms that have prevailed throughout most of history. First, when science and culture clash, science loses. Thus, Galileo repudiates the Earth's motion; Dr. Semmelweis is so reviled for believing in germs that he kills himself; evolution is still not taught as established fact, or else not taught at all.

Second norm, in the words of Nobel Laureate Gary Becker: "When culture runs up against economic trends, usually economics win out." Or, for those of you who require graphics to grasp a concept:

SCIENCE < CULTURE < MONEY

Our current sorry state, however, is a perfect storm of culture and economics united to drown science, law, and other rational pursuits. For over fifty years, the United States has been losing manufacturing, industrial, and agricultural jobs, and replacing them with jobs based on information, consumer acquisition, and services such as health and government. These jobs respond to cultural shifts in a way that, say, the manufacture of steel did not. A car needs to be drivable for anyone to buy it. A turnip needs to be planted and harvested. A bra needs to hold up the ta-ta's. But a service economy, less pragmatically defined, responds to whatever services or information are requested. So does government, in order to secure votes. The health sector never guaranteed that all would be cured, or even substantially helped.

This means that right now, money is unusually responsive to popular culture. Popular culture, perhaps in response to the worldwide depression, has gone non-rational. Thus the proliferation of psychic fairs, exorcisms, curse-lifting boutiques, miracle workers, covens, faith healing, séances, "wars" against demons, potion shops, agencies locating guardian angels or personal totems or sacred lakes, and psychologists willing to help you remember that in a past life you were Cleopatra. Science, the reasoning goes, has failed to either give us our daily bread or to deliver us from spiritual meaninglessness. So we look elsewhere for help.

With what results?

Productivity per capita has fallen to its lowest point in a hundred years.

Courts are clogged with cases that judges once would have dismissed as frivolous, if not insane.

Child Protection agencies are so overburdened with allegations of cult practices endangering children, some true but most merely filed by competing cultish believers, that investigators are swamped. Tens of thousands of legitimate abuse or neglect cases therefore go uninvestigated.

Academic achievement in our high schools, slipping for decades in comparison with other developed countries, is now surpassed by most of the Third World.

The American political process has become so balkanized by third-party factions that few state legislatures can get anything productive accomplished at all. This US Congress has passed the least amount of legislation of any congress ever.

This is not to say that there may not be some truth in the Age of Imagination—in the larger concept, *not* in the violent cults. Perhaps there is more "out there" besides the rational world. Perhaps unseen forces do exist in the universe. I wouldn't know. But this I do know:

Too many have mistaken a piece of the truth for the whole. And we are all suffering the consequences.

Hannah rushed through her bedroom door into the kitchen, dropping her tablet case on the table and shrugging herself into the jacket of her summer-weight business suit. She glanced at Annabel. "News flash: Nobody reads editorials anymore. Especially not ones with a snotty attitude and dependent clauses."

"News flash," Annabel said. "I do. It's good, Hannah. Do you want some coffee?"

"If it's ready right now. I have to be at a town meeting in twenty minutes."

"It's only six-thirty in the morning!"

"I know. Aren't you going to be late for school? No, wait—you dropped out of school."

"Don't start," Annabel warned.

"I would start if I had time. You're drifting, Annabel."

"What's the town meeting about?"

"Zoning," Hannah said, standing as she gulped her coffee.

"Zoning for what?"

"You won't believe it. Some idiot wants to build a past-life discovery center in a residential district, and the even greater idiots on the board want to let him."

Annabel didn't ask why this was a bad idea; she didn't want to set Hannah off on a rant. She also didn't want to open any discussion of what she was going to do today on her day off. Fortunately, Hannah had no time to ask.

Annabel reheated her coffee, dressed, and puttered around the kitchen. A two-bedroom in a secure neighborhood, it was cheerful with the yellow curtains she had hung, redolent with the meals she cooked. Hannah said that Annabel had the skills and temperament of a different historical era, when they would have been more valued in a woman. Annabel thought this was probably true but not very comforting. She'd spent much of her life wanting to be someone else: Hannah, her friend Becca, her father, Keith.

Don't think about Keith.

She walked to the train station. It was only 7:30, but the sun beat down. On the platform, sweating in her thin dress, she saw a boy about her age, SLA patch on his shoulder, walk slowly toward her with a dog on a choke chain. The commuters, fewer each month, stepped away from him.

Were dogs allowed on the train? Annabel didn't know. This dog was big, a Doberman or Great Dane or something, with a deep muscular chest. Brown fur, brown eyes, brownish teeth: a monochromatic shadow, pacing slow and stately beside the boy. But at least the dog's eyes looked normal. The boy's eyes scared her. His head, shaved, was bare—no N-cap. Was he on a street drug?

They stopped beside an old woman sitting on a bench, canvas shopping bag at her feet, a loaf of Italian bread peeking from the top. The dog ignored the bread. He sniffed at the old woman, then paced on. Behind them, she spat on the platform floor.

The dog must be sniffing for drugs or explosives. But that boy was no cop.

They reached Annabel. Up close, the boy's face looked even scarier, as if it were made of wood, not flesh. When his eyes fell on Annabel, however, his gaze softened slightly. Even through her anxiety, that surprised her—it was usually Hannah, not Annabel, who provoked that look from males.

The dog sniffed at her. Annabel's heart began to swell and thump, but the dog paced on.

Farther up the platform, the dog sniffed at a woman talking into her wrister. The dog went as rigid as the boy's face, snarled, and lunged. It didn't reach the woman; the boy pulled hard on the choke chain and the dog jerked backward. But it kept snarling, the woman screamed, and five young people exploded from the stairway down to the platform. All wore SLA patches. They surrounded the woman and began jabbering at her, crowding her, thrusting pamphlets at her. Annabel heard the words "demon" and "cleanse" before the train screeched into the station and stopped. Two men farther down the platform rushed to the woman, knocking aside the girl who was closest to the woman, almost on top of her, yelling and waving a pamphlet. The train door opened and Annabel got on, feeling as if she had been the one assaulted.

The SLA followers hadn't hurt the woman, hadn't even touched her. Still…and a dog "trained" to sniff out supposed demons! Was that possible? Were demons possible?

Annabel had tried, often, to think about this, to think about anything not rational, a task made more difficult because of Hannah's uber-contempt and Annabel's innate fairness. The best she could come up with was that irrational phenomena couldn't be proved but couldn't be disproved either, so the verdict wasn't in yet. She knew that this wishy-washy conclusion would satisfy nobody, certainly not Hannah. It didn't even satisfy Annabel. But she could live with an ambiguity that, apparently, most people could not. Her solution, also not really satisfying, was mostly to not think about it, which was her solution to most difficulties.

Hannah's voice in her head: *"You're drifting, Annabel."*

Well, she wasn't drifting this morning. She had a destination.

The little house on Barlow Street looked even worse than last week. Grass and weeds were higher, a shutter had come off its hinges on one side, and some kid had bashed in the light over the front steps, raining shards onto the stoop. Annabel unlocked the door and went in.

"Mom?"

"Annabel! How nice to see you!"

As if she didn't see Annabel every Thursday. Unlike the outside of her house, Julia Sevley looked trim and neat. The living room was vacuumed, the breakfast dishes washed, the latest plastic container of delivery groceries in the process of being unpacked on the kitchen table. Every window in the house was covered with curtains, slatted blinds, or both. Although recovered from her divorce, Annabel's mother had not left the house in two years. If she so much as approached the opened front door, she began to sweat, shake, and breathe so fast that Annabel had stopped trying to take her mother outside.

They went through the Thursday ritual: breakfast, chat about nothing, two games of Scrabble on a board so old-fashioned that it used plastic tiles for the letters. Annabel reported that Hannah was fine, she herself was fine, the new apartment was fine. Anything else brought Julia to the brink of an anxiety too acute for Annabel to deal with. She knew; she'd tried.

At noon they ate lunch, then Annabel left. Clouds had rolled in, piling into anvil-shaped thunderheads. The air felt sticky and thick, like walking through wet cotton. The train station was a mile away. Annabel sighed, started walking, and then stopped.

A blue light shone from the upstairs window next door.

Annabel blinked. Mr. Brywood had died less than a year after his wife of, perhaps, a broken heart. Keith had been sent away to live with an aunt in New York. But Hannah said that Keith had inherited the house and a modest trust had kept up the taxes and paid a service to keep the place in repair until Keith chose to sell it. Apparently he never had, and the house had stood empty for two years. Keith's birthday was in July; he must be eighteen now.

Annabel climbed the porch and rang the bell. It didn't sound; the repair company must not be very good. She tried the doorknob. The door opened.

Dust lay so thick on the floor, furniture, and stairs that they all looked covered with fine ash, as if Vesuvius had erupted in this old tract house. Annabel called, "Keith?" No answer. She climbed the stairs.

Danger. The organisms felt it in Annabel's increased heart rate, skin moisture, adrenal output. In three years, they had made tremendous strides in both interpreting the behavior of their host and in controlling their own. However, the only part of Annabel that they had succeeded in controlling were the pheromones she gave off, which bore some resemblance to their own chemical signaling method.

As Annabel mounted the stairs, they rushed to protect their host in the only way they could. Undetected by her, her skin began to give off clouds of pheromones. Fashioned more or less after molecules of oxytocin, they were designed to soothe and calm any human within olfactory range. This was the second time today the entity had activated the pheromones. That was unusual.

Unusual was not good.

"Keith?" Annabel pushed open the bedroom door.

He lay on his back on the floor in a pool of his own urine, giggling. All his bones were visible through the taut sack of his pasty skin. His collarbones, sharp as chisels, pointed at the ceiling. The neural cap, a heavy mesh that didn't even try to look inconspicuous, covered most of his shaved head.

Fury tore through Annabel. Gagging at the stench in the room, she tore the N-cap from Keith's head, taking part of his skin with it. Unlike any version she'd ever seen before, this N-cap sunk tiny electrodes directly into the skull. Keith screamed and tried to focus his eyes. He couldn't, and passed out.

"Keith!" His breath came in irregular pants. His lips began to turn blue. Annabel raised her wrister and called Emergency. Then she crouched beside him—no pulse. Over and over she pressed on his chest, not knowing if CPR would save him or would crack his fragile, malnourished ribs.

He was still alive when the medics took him away, after first slapping so many patches on him that he looked like an Amish quilt. Annabel answered as many questions as she could, which weren't many, until the medics let her go.

"You're lucky we got here at all," a woman in scrubs told her. "We happened to just be around the corner, called to a guy who didn't make it. Otherwise, your friend would be a corpse."

"But—"

"No 'buts' about it, kid. Too many emergencies. Too many stupid Keiths." The woman shrugged and turned away.

Annabel took the train back to Boston. She needed to go somewhere that made sense, somewhere life wasn't either agoraphobic or addicted, falsely cheerful or willfully suicidal. The Center would still be open for hours yet. At the train station she took the T to Canberra Street.

"Annabel! Isn't today your day off?"

"Yes, but I got bored."

Roberta raised her eyebrows. She was a good day-care administrator, but not particularly good with children, nor particularly warm. Seth, Annabel's co-worker, was. Annabel greeted him in the infants' section, where he was diapering a shrieking six-month-old. She picked up an infant just starting to fuss in her crib. The baby quieted.

"I don't know how you do that," Seth said. "They always turn so good the second you show up!" His child continued to shriek.

"Here, let's trade before Brandon wakes the whole room!"

Seth traded gladly. Annabel finished cleaning Brandon, diapered him, and settled with him into a rocker. The baby quieted. He wore only the diaper; the AC had been turned off again for late payment of the bill, since half the parents who used the Canberra Street Center were late with their fees. If they had the money at all. This part of Boston was filled with working poor. Annabel had been here for three months; Hannah thought she still worked in the job Hannah had gotten her in the day care center at Harvard. But Annabel liked it better here. The children needed her more.

She held the baby up on her shoulder, rocked him, and sang softly. Brandon's eyelids began to droop. The sweet baby smell rose from the back of his neck. The soft skin of his powdered belly pressed against the exposed cleavage of Annabel's summer dress.

The baby fell asleep. Annabel rocked, and sang, and soothed herself as well as Brandon. But the horror of what Keith had become—had *allowed* himself to become, she wasn't letting him off the hook on that—would not leave her mind.

Another host! But there was not much time; there never was. Special cells were sent racing toward the surface of the primary host. The entity was much more efficient at this now; it understood the environment and had evolved to utilize it. Unlike that first, dangerous time, transfer needed only about ten minutes.

The transfer cells left Annabel's skin through microtubules evolved for this purpose. They oozed from her and onto Brandon. There they exuded a lytic chemical that softened the epidermis, comparatively tough even on a baby, and began to burrow in.

VI: January, 2028

PAUL APLEY DIDN'T LIKE his research assistant.

He supposed that he should be glad he had one at all. Months of solo legwork had begun to show enough results that the CDC, perpetually short-handed and underfunded, had grudgingly assigned him a post-doc. Emily Zimmer was bright, organized, and hard-working. She was also arrogant, although that alone wouldn't have put Paul off. Arrogance was sometimes a useful trait in an epidemiologist; it indicated faith in one's own work even if the results seemed weird. Sometimes arrogance could sustain a researcher through the inevitable unpopularity when those results upset other people's theories, or budgets, or lives. During the Tashman Fever epidemic four years ago, only scientific arrogance had been enough to drive New York politicians to burn down three square blocks of hopelessly infected Brooklyn real estate.

So arrogance wasn't what bothered Paul about Emily. Rather, it was a kind of slipperiness, a slyness. Most post-docs were frank about their goals and ambitions. Emily always slid the conversation away from her own aspirations, plans, and beliefs. Post-docs were always submitting resumes, asking for recommendations, discussing permanent positions that they—sometimes unrealistically—hoped to land. Emily never did, and she thwarted all of Paul's offers of help. Was it natural reticence, which he was being an asshole to try to breach? Or connections he didn't know about, so that her future was already assured? Maybe. So why did it bother him? He knew she'd grown up desperately poor; that she was willing to talk about. Only scholarships and insanely ceaseless work had gotten her an education. Often she threw out barbs about "trust fund babies."

And yet much as she envied the rich, she also felt disdain for the poor people she interviewed, a disdain not evident while she was in the field (or she couldn't have gotten so much good data), but expressed in remarks to Paul in their shared office, which was so small he couldn't get away from her. "People end up at the socioeconomic level they deserve," she'd once told Paul, and brushed aside his protests as soft-headed soft-heartedness.

On a gray afternoon she came into their office and said, "I put the Joslyn data into the Link program." Water puddled off her boots: Boston had had one of its increasingly rare snowfalls. Paul, born in Georgia, thought snow was too cold and too inconvenient. Emily, from Minnesota, barely noticed it. "I think we might actually have something, Paul."

He opened his laptop and brought up the Link program. A three-dimensional and infinitely more sophisticated version of a spreadsheet combined with a flow chart, it was an intricate, three-D holo with beams of light in different colors connecting different kinds of data points in different ways. Emily had added information from her latest interviews with the parents, doctors, relatives, and babysitters of Brandon Joslyn. Five months ago Brandon, then eight months old, had collapsed into a month-long coma and emerged, like all the rest of the babies, perfectly fine and with no discernible physical markers that might indicate the cause of the coma.

For the first time, one of Link's light beams had thickened past random chance.

The children whose data glowed on Link all lived in different parts of Boston. One infant was the child of a Harvard professor, another of a heroin addict, a large number from parents who comprised the working poor. They were Christian, Jewish, Hindu, Muslim, witches, SLA, New Miraclists, atheists, reincarnationists, renegade Amish, and Church of the Expanded Holy Consciousness. Some would allow blood samples and access to medical records, some would not. Paul and Emily had spent a lot of time creating family charts, looking for a common genetic marker.

They had been looking in the wrong places.

The children had attended day care centers in Roxbury, Chelsea, Cambridge, Beacon Hill, downtown. Now it turned out that a single day-care provider had worked in all those places. She hadn't been obvious at first because in some of the cases she had left her job as much as a month before a child went into a coma, and a month was a long time for incubation of infant diseases. And yet, there was Link, glowing out her name with a coefficient of significance higher than chance. Annabel Lee Sevley.

"There's more," Emily said, closing the master and bringing up a link from news archives, "although it may not be significant. Our Annabel was once all over the news. She fell down a crevasse in the Rocky Mountains when she was not quite three, and there was a big splashy effort to save her."

Paul frowned. "I can't see that that's relevant."

"It could be. You don't know." Most conversations with Emily felt like low-level combats. "Maybe Annabel picked up some kind of virus down there, the way index-case Charles Monet picked up Ebola in Kitum Cave in 1980."

"Nobody's even sure that's the way it happened. But you're right that this girl is someone of interest. Let's go talk to her. I just hope she's not a witch or an angel or something."

"I just hope she doesn't smell bad," Emily said. "So many of them do."

Annabel had visited her mother, arriving in the afternoon—her new job gave her a new schedule—and staying for dinner. When she emerged from the shuttered, curtained house, snow was falling. The flakes were huge, each one a delicate, slowly drifting miracle that seemed to take an eon to reach the ground. Snow lay over the pavement, the dead weeds, the dreary little street. The cold air stung Annabel's cheeks.

She laughed out loud. The laugh died, replaced by something more solemn. It was so quiet, so fresh and innocent, especially after her mother's stuffy house, where no windows or curtains were ever opened. Annabel started walking, her shoes leaving indentations in the snow. She walked not toward the train station but in the opposite direction. A few blocks away, an open field had never been developed by the company that bought it just before the world economy collapsed. As children, Annabel and Keith and their friends had played soccer here. The street lights had long since been vandalized and the field was unlit, but Annabel had a small flashlight in her purse. She made her way to the center of the field.

It was an unbroken stretch of white, pristine and lovely. Gradually the snow stopped. In the east the clouds parted and a section of sky was visible, thick with bright winter stars: Rigel, Betelgeuse, Sirius, Aldebaran.

Something came over Annabel that she had never before experienced: a feeling of holiness. It touched her, or she it. *This*, she thought, and didn't know what she meant, until she did. *This lovely, lovely world that is more than I know.* More what? It didn't matter. The feeling was enough.

And then, it wasn't. She felt the stars tug at her, and for a moment it was almost as if she could go there. If she just willed herself hard enough, if she just tried... She was part of that vast starry expanse and with every molecule of her being, she wanted to belong more closely to the mystery behind the veil, wanted...

A car raced across the field, shattering the silence.

Annabel switched off her flashlight, but she was too late. The teenagers had seen her. They piled out of the car, which was very old and painted with multi-colored zigzags. Two boys and two girls. No SLA patches.

"Well, well," one of the girls said, lurching out of the car and hanging onto the hood for support. "And who are *you*?"

Should she run? They were clearly drunk. But the boys could still probably catch her, and anyway she couldn't outrun the car. They might run her over.

"My name is Annabel." She tried to sound like Hannah, firm and authoritative, and knew she failed.

"Nice boots, Annabel," the girl said. "Give them to me."

The boys lounged against the fenders, enjoying this. The second girl circled behind Annabel.

She took off her boots and threw them at the girl. Immediately snow drenched her socks. She shivered.

"Well, thank you so much, Annabel," the girl mocked. "Now give me your wallet."

She drew it from her purse and threw it.

"Fine, just fucking fine. Now that pretty coat."

Annabel stripped it off. A strange impulse came to her: *Walk toward them.* She didn't.

One of the boys shifted his weight on the fender. The girl holding Annabel's boots, wallet, and coat said silkily, "You want her, Tom?"

The other girl spoke for the first time, her words slurred but her tone dangerous. "You screw her, Tom, and I'll cut 'em off with a rusty spoon."

The first girl laughed. "How about you, Jed? She's pretty enough."

The second boy, grinning, started toward Annabel. She started to scream and run. The second girl caught her and they both crashed to the snow. Jed straddled Annabel and put his hand on her breast.

A second later he pulled it away. In the glow from the car's headlights, he looked puzzled. For a long moment nobody spoke. Then the second girl got to her feet and moved away, and Jed also rose.

"Fuck, she ain't pretty enough after all."

"But—" said the first girl.

"Shut your trap, Jasmine. This is boring. C'mon, let's go."

"I don't—"

"I said let's go!"

The four climbed into the car, the first girl still arguing, and the car sped back across the field.

Annabel leapt to her feet and ran toward the street, shivering and sobbing. It wasn't until she'd reached her mother's front porch that the question formed in her mind: *What just happened there?*

Her mother peered through the peephole, flung open the front door, and immediately jumped away from it. "Annabel! What happened!"

"Some kids…I'm all right, just cold…" She slammed the door.

Her mother locked and double-bolted it before whirling to face her daughter. "Are you sure you're all right? I'll call the police! You're frozen, take off those wet things, I'll get towels and a blanket…"

And then, in a mixture of despair and triumph, "I always told you girls it's too dangerous to go outside!"

The chemical equivalent of panic spread among the network of cells that was the organism. Most still resided in or on Annabel's nerve cells. Some had become organelles, fully as complex as those within the host's own cells. Some were free-living in brain tissues. Chemical and electrical signaling flew among the components of the vast network.

The host's single defense had preserved her. But just barely. The attackers of the host had almost not been soothed enough by the cloud of pheromones the entity had released. And the host could not have outrun them or outfought them or harmed them. The entity was going to need more defenses, more under its own control.

It had to further change Annabel.

Hannah answered her apartment door, expecting a pizza. No matter how psycho everything else got, she thought, the pizza business flourisheth, yea and verily.

It wasn't the pizza delivery. A man and woman stood there, snow melting onto the hallway. "Annabel Lee Sevley?"

"Who wants to know?"

The man showed her I.D. "We're from the Centers for Disease Control. I'm Dr. Paul Apley, and this is Dr. Emily Zimmer. May we come in?"

The CDC. That usually meant disease, even plague. Hannah gripped the doorknob more tightly. "What's this about?"

"Are you Annabel Sevley?"

"I'm Hannah Sevley, her sister and legal guardian." Not true, guardianship had never been transferred from their mother and Annabel had turned eighteen, but you got more information that way. "What's this about?"

"An investigation that the CDC is conducting."

She wasn't going to get more unless she let them inside. "First I'm going to verify your credentials."

The man smiled. Hannah closed the door, made the call, and opened it again. Her belly felt light, as if it might float up into her throat. But she kept her voice crisp, professional.

"Sit down. Then tell me why you want to see Annabel."

He gazed at her, and Hannah saw the moment he decided that she wasn't taking any evasive bullshit. He said, "We've been running an investigation on a condition spreading throughout children in the Boston area. We think your sister may be a carrier."

"A 'condition,' not a disease? What condition? And why do you suspect Annabel?"

"She's the only person we can identify who's been in contact with all the affected children."

"Circumstantial evidence."

"Yes, of course." His tone was soothing, which infuriated Hannah. "But we would like to talk to Annabel."

"She's not here. You can talk to me, I'm not only her sister but also her lawyer."

Paul Apley shifted his weight on the shabby sofa, which Hannah had been intending to replace but hadn't had time. "She doesn't need a lawyer, Ms. Sevley, and she's not being accused of anything. But if she is a transmitter of this condition—"

"Which is what?"

The other doctor, the snotty-looking woman, spoke for the first time. "Month-long infant coma with no after-effects, similar and perhaps identical to the one your sister suffered after she was pulled from that mountain crevasse fifteen years ago."

Hannah said evenly, "Annabel had been underground for nearly three days. She almost lost a toe to frostbite. Trauma and injury caused the coma, the doctors told my parents so at the time, and Annabel came out of the coma with no lasting effects whatsoever."

"I believe you," Paul Apley said. If he had smiled at her while he said it, or looked into her eyes, Hannah would have thrown them both out of the apartment. But instead he ran his hand distractedly through his hair, and his face had the scrunched, eye-unfocused look of a man thinking intently. He wasn't trying to charm Hannah; he was searching for answers.

What if something was genuinely wrong with Annabel?

Hannah said, "Please tell me about this alleged condition. What you know for sure, what you suspect, and what evidence you have linking it to Annabel."

He did, and Hannah listened harder than she ever had to any deposition, any criminal confession, any string of precedents that she might have to undermine or disprove.

Annabel insisted on going home. Her mother protested and argued and wept, but in the end she had come up with money for a taxi. Her mother's finances were a mystery to Annabel, although she might have inherited something from Annabel's father, who had died a year ago. Or had his second wife gotten it all?

At any rate, there was a taxi and Annabel, wrapped in an old coat of her mother's that was too big for her, plus three layers of socks because all of Julia's shoes were too small, climbed out of the cab in downtown Boston. She let herself into the apartment to find two strangers sitting with Hannah.

Her first impression was amazement that Hannah, that workaholic, was actually sitting, and with visitors instead of her laptop or tablet. Annabel's second thought was that maybe the man was a boyfriend. But then, why the girl? She was too old to be his daughter; she looked about Hannah's age, and the man in his early forties.

"Annabel," Hannah said, in a tone she didn't recognize, "this is Dr. Paul Apley and Dr. Emily Zimmer. They're from the CDC. They want to ask you some questions, and as your lawyer, I want you to answer only when I say you may."

Annabel blinked. Lawyer? CDC? Was there...oh God, was there a plague? Was Hannah infected?

"Don't be frightened, Annabel," Dr. Apley said, at the same moment that Hannah said, "Where are your shoes? And why are you wearing Mom's old coat? Haven't you been at work?"

Annabel said, "Could I please have a cup of hot tea?"

The doctors told their story, and Annabel told hers. The incident in the snowy field was quickly disposed of; Annabel hadn't wanted her mother to call the police and her mother hadn't, not wanting strangers in the house, and after all Annabel hadn't been hurt and the cops probably wouldn't ever catch the punks anyway. Annabel left out what she had experienced while looking up at the stars. Hannah would just say that spiritual feelings were archaic wish-fulfillment.

Then the doctors talked. It became, Annabel saw, a kind of contest, with both the doctors and Hannah trying to obtain as much information as possible, while giving away as little as possible.

Despite that, Annabel finally realized that the doctors were saying that she had somehow caused babies at day-care centers to go into a coma.

"I didn't!"

"Not intentionally," Dr. Apley said. "We know that. But Annabel, if you're a carrier, a person who is immune to the condition herself but passing it on, then surely you'd want to know that?"

"Well, yes," Annabel said.

Hannah scowled at her. "We are in no way admitting that Annabel is a carrier."

"I said 'if,'" Dr. Apley said.

Annabel said, "But how did I get this…'condition'?"

"We don't know," Dr. Apley said.

Dr. Zimmer said, "Most emerging diseases are zoonotic."

"What does that mean?"

"It means that the pathogen lives in a different animal but has jumped species to infect humans."

Dr. Apley said, "It may be premature to say that. Annabel, we'd like to run some tests."

Hannah said, "Annabel has had a physical every year of her life. Nothing abnormal has ever been found." This wasn't strictly true but Annabel, still shocked, didn't correct Hannah.

Dr. Apley said, "Physicals are gross-level checks for infections, abnormalities, and the kinds of diseases that leave markers in blood and urine. I doubt that Annabel has ever had so much as an fMRI since she was a child—have you, Annabel?"

Annabel said nothing; she wasn't sure what an fMRI was.

"What we want to do is far more subtle and thorough. Our advanced tests won't harm Annabel, won't hurt, and will carry no cost to you. And, Ms. Sevley, if we truly suspect she is a danger to public health, I know that *you* know that we can get a court order for quarantine."

"You don't have anything that comes close to probable cause."

"I can get the court order under Massachusetts General Law, Chapter 111."

"You mean," Hannah said, "that you can find a judge who's either such a hyper-rationalist that he holds medicine in holy awe, or such an Age of Imagination sympathizer that he doesn't want to take a chance she's possessed by a demon."

Hannah and Dr. Apley stared at each other. Neither blinked. Annabel said, "I will have the tests."

Hannah turned to her. "Annabel—"

"No, this is my decision. I want to know. If I put babies into a coma, I want to know, even though they're all okay now." To her horror, tears overflowed.

Dr. Zimmer gave a quick roll of her eyes. Hannah clenched her fists. Dr. Apley passed Annabel a tissue. And there came over Annabel a huge, tidal-wave-sized feeling that she should not do this: *No no no no no no.*

She pushed down the feeling. She had to know. She, Annabel.

The tests were carried out at Massachusetts General, where Annabel had a quarantine room "as a precaution." Hannah, subjected to a much smaller array of tests, insisted on staying with her as much as possible, on calling frequently when she couldn't, and on repeating endlessly that Annabel should say nothing to anybody. This made for a boring three days when Annabel wasn't being scanned, prodded, sampled, or examined. So many bits of her were taken away for analysis that she marveled anything was left.

At night, sleeping in her hospital bed with Hannah in a cot across the room, Annabel dreamed. She had always had vague, highly colored dreams, and now they became even vaguer and more highly colored. She usually woke with the strong feeling that she'd been somewhere else, someplace constantly shifting and speeding and busy, someplace utterly alien and yet familiar.

Annabel sought information on the Internet about the children she'd cared for. Usually there was a spate of new-born pictures, then nothing. She had only been working in day care for a year. The children had no Internet presence yet, and the parents were usually poor. The exceptions, two of them, dated from her brief job at the Harvard University Day

Care Center, where Annabel had loved the kids (she always loved the kids) but not the parents. Two babies, James Whitman and Parminder Bhatnagar, had fallen into comas after Annabel left. Parents, grandparents, and siblings had blogged about it. Everybody continued to blog and to post pictures, and both children were now adorable and healthy toddlers. It was ridiculous to think anything was wrong with them.

It was ridiculous to think anything was wrong with herself.

Wasn't it?

The entity knew what was happening. Pieces of itself removed—not many, but not good. And nothing it could do to stop it. Its only defense so far was clouds of soothing pheromones. But changes were underway.

On each of the host's nerve cells sat sacs with membranes made of fat, sugars, and protein. The sacs stored various molecules, each one a nitrogen atom surrounded by two hydrogen atoms tethered to the molecule by a short, distinctive chain of carbons. The entity had learned that these monoamines could be released by dissolving the sacs, modulating the activity of the brain.

In addition, each of these monoamines set off cascades of interlocking molecular interactions throughout the entire host. So did other substances stored in different tissues. The cascades could be triggered, intensified, or interrupted at various points. The entity now knew enough about the host, and the host's environment, to create mechanisms that would do that, and the raw materials were all to hand.

The entity did not "think" this, in human terms. Its consciousness was too different. But consciousness there was, aimed at long-term survival, and capable of action focused to that universal, all-important end.

It needed to protect the host from the outside world.
Urgently it set to work.

"A parasite," the doctors said. "Of an unknown type we've never seen before."

Hannah reached for Annabel's hand, but Annabel looked calm, if pale. Actually, Hannah felt calmer than she would have expected. She attributed this to her courtroom experience. Her recorder was on, and her wrister ready for notes. She said quietly, "Is it in any way life-threatening?"

One of the doctors—there were two from Mass General in addition to Paul and Emily—said, "Not that we can tell. Annabel is in perfect health."

Paul said, "You have to understand, both of you, that we're in the dark here. The thing is, the parasite is an entirely different type from anything known. It's carbon-based, certainly, but it seems to contain neither DNA nor RNA, and what it does seem to contain are some unknown structures along with some analogues to human cells. It resides mostly, but not exclusively, on nerve and brain cells and in the cerebrospinal fluid. An MRI shows nodularity along nerves. Electron microscopes show a chain of bead-like structures with motile flagella, but not like anything ever observed before. They won't stain properly or—"

"*Wait*," Hannah said, more sharply, "In her *brain*?"

"Yes."

Annabel's fingers tightened on Hannah's. Annabel said, "Will it...will it change my brain?"

"We don't know." Paul ran his hand through his hair in the distracted gesture that Hannah had found herself watching for. "Parasites are...can be...tricky."

"I know," Annabel said, surprising Hannah. "I've been reading about them while I'm here. There's one you can get from cat shit that makes rats unafraid of cats, makes them actually attracted to the smell of cat pee, so that the cat can eat the rat and the parasite can get back into the cat."

"*T. gondii*," Paul said, looking unhappy.

"And it affects people, too," Annabel continued steadily. "A lot of research says that it makes humans more willing to take risks by cranking up the production of dopamine. Flu makes people become more sociable while it's in the contagious stage, because the flu wants to be spread around to—"

"Flu doesn't 'want' anything," Emily said disdainfully. "It's a *virus*."

Annabel continued as if Emily hadn't spoken. "—infect as many people as possible. People in the last stages of syphilis crave sex more, to also spread the disease. Syphilis affects dopamine, too, like the cat-shit parasite. And like N-caps."

Hannah said, "Annie, sweetie, I don't think N-caps have anything to do with this."

Annabel looked hard at Paul. "Did I pass this parasite on to babies? Have you tested any of the kids that went into a coma?"

"Not yet. You're first, so we know what we're looking for."

"But you will test them?"

"All those whose parents agree." Emily had already started the visits to obtain permission. "Meanwhile, Annabel, it might be best if you remain here in the hospital."

"No," Hannah said swiftly. Here she was on firm ground. "By Chapter iii, Section 6, quarantine can only be imposed if a disease is 'declared dangerous to the public health' by the Public Health Commissioner. Annabel's alleged parasite has not been so declared and does not meet the criteria to be so declared."

Paul said mildly, "I think it does, Ms. Sevley. The condition is communicable, Annabel poses a risk of infecting others, and the commissioner will issue a declaration if the CDC tells her to."

"You would have to demonstrate a significant risk to others, and you haven't even got hard medical evidence that those other children are carrying the alleged parasite."

"Nonetheless, the Commissioner can take any quarantine action that she 'deems advisable for the protection of public health.' Massachusetts grants the PHD pretty broad discretionary powers, as you know."

Hannah's respect for Paul rose, along with her dislike. "You need a magistrate to issue an *ex parte* motion to take Annabel."

"I can get one."

"If you—"

"*Wait*," Annabel said. "Everybody, just wait!"

Everybody waited except Hannah, who said, "Don't say anything, Annabel."

Annabel ignored her sister. "Dr. Apley, if I stay at our apartment and don't go to work—don't go anywhere at all, just stay home—is that enough?"

Home isolation was actually what Hannah had been ultimately bargaining for, but Annabel had gotten there first. You never asked directly for what you really wanted; you began by showing that you were willing to fight, so that when you did compromise, the other side thought it had won something. But Annabel didn't know that legal strategy.

Neither, apparently, did Paul Apley. He said, "Yes, I think that would be all right, as long as you're monitored for compliance."

"Maybe I could wear one of those ankle bracelet things," Annabel said, once again giving away the store before negotiation. Hannah stifled her sigh.

"Okay," Paul said. "Annabel, I know this isn't easy for you."

"No," Annabel agreed. "But now I want to ask some questions. Will you answer them truthfully?"

"Yes," Paul said, even while the two physicians shifted their weight uneasily on the sofa, and Emily frowned.

Annabel said, "Can you get this parasite out of me?"

Hannah held her breath. Paul hesitated, but he answered. "Probably not. Nerve-attached and brain-diffused conditions are notoriously difficult to treat. Anything strong enough to kill them also kills the patient."

"Did I infect Hannah?"

"No. Her tests show no sign of the organisms."

"Will this parasite eventually kill me?"

"Annabel, we have no idea what it will do. But my best guess is no. Parasites that kill their host also kill themselves. You've had this a long time, and you're in excellent health. I don't think it will harm you, or at least I can't see any evolutionary advantage it would gain by doing so."

"You said it's in my nerves and brain. Is it influencing my behavior?"

He threw out both arms, palms upwards. "How would I know? I don't know what your behavior would have been like without it."

Hannah blinked, unused to such honesty from the opposition.

"Well," Annabel said, with a sudden and completely un-expected smile, "if I start acting weird, you probably can't distinguish it from everybody else out there."

Paul laughed. Hannah, to her own shocked surprise, laughed along with him.

The entity, utilizing all the resources of its own peculiar collective mind, made swift progress in controlling Annabel's concentrations of serotonin, dopamine, norepinephrine, adrenalin, cortisol, and much more. It would not allow the host to be endangered again.

VII: April, 2030

SPRING AGAIN IN BOSTON. Daffodils, hyacinths, tulips were in full bloom, roses in bud. Annabel grew flowers in pots on the third-floor apartment balcony, so many flowers that there was room for only one chair, which she sat in for many hours each day with her tablet on her lap. Hannah had resumed her punishing work schedule, although she tried to get home as often as possible. It wasn't very often.

"Funny, isn't it," she emailed her mother, "to feel lonesome when I'm inhabited by a whole colony?"

No. Delete the message. Her mother was already upset at Annabel's condition (only vaguely explained to her as "chronic infection"), but not upset enough to fight her agoraphobia and visit. Hannah was openly scornful of this. For Annabel, her mother's absence, her sister's absence, her general isolation, fueled a growing and bewildered rage.

Why this? Why me?

She spent hours telling herself there was no answer to this question. Random chance hit everybody; the parasites were not bothering her; Paul would find a way to cure her. She didn't believe any of it. She was nineteen years old, she felt isolated and angry, and her mother wouldn't even come to visit. Although was it her mother she wanted to see again, or was it that open field where under starlight she had experienced her one and only approach to a mystic, other-worldly, holy experience?

And had the experience actually been hers, or the parasites' within her?

Her "termites." She was a house with termites all through it, hidden deep in the walls and floors and roof beams. Her whole life Annabel had wanted to be somebody else, and now she was, and it still wasn't really her. In some moods that struck her as funny, but not very often.

She taught herself to meditate, following tablet presentations by Buddhist monks, hoping to experience again what had happened in that snowy field. Meditation never even brought her close.

It would have been better, she knew, if she left the apartment more often, made friends, took some classes. The monitor she wore would let her do that, with some restrictions. But she mostly hadn't, not for over a year and a half, because of the babies. Now and then she and Hannah went to plays, movies, restaurants, hiking trips, whenever Hannah had time. She'd even gone out a few times with Emily, Paul's research assistant, whom Annabel didn't really like. But mostly she stayed home alone, fighting her growing fury, because of the babies.

There went one now.

Three stories below, two women pushed a high-wheeled, expensive-looking English pram along the street. Annabel had watched them before: Jane and Melissa with their daughter Pia. Jane was the biological mother. The women had married two years ago; Pia was nine months old. Melissa had recently joined a coven and Jane didn't like that. Sometimes they argued over money. Annabel had listened to them, watched them, all winter, staring hungrily at Pia.

She must never hold a baby again. It wasn't even her who wanted to hold it, it was the termites inside her—

Angry tears sprang to her eyes. Annabel dashed them away. She watched Pia's pram turn the corner, resisting the urge to drop a flowerpot down onto the sidewalk just to hear it shatter. She'd done that once before. It only meant going outside to clean it up, to apologize to old Mrs. Lucurcio on the ground floor, to either buy a new pot or do with one fewer of the few bright, colorful things in her stupid life.

It wasn't fair.

Annabel rattled around the kitchen, making herself a cup of herbal tea she didn't really want. Soothing feelings began to take her, and she didn't want that, either. Paul had tested the air around Annabel when she got upset. The parasites gave off some kind of weird pheromones that calmed everybody down, including Annabel. Fuck that! Sometimes all she wanted was for the whole thing to be over.

The doorbell rang.

Annabel stopped rattling the teakettle. Hannah never rang; Paul and Emily always called before they came over. Mrs. Lucurcio? Cops? There had been another SLA flash mob on the street the night before, mostly peaceful except for some shoving and shouting, but maybe the police were asking questions anyway. Or it might, finally, be the press.

That Paul had kept Annabel and the other children out of the press was a sort of miracle. It had taken a deftly wielded combination of cajolery, promises, and threats. The threats, legal in nature, had come from Hannah. She had joined with him in pointing out to the parents of the twenty-three children Annabel had infected the realities of the situation. No siblings had been infected; Paul theorized that they were too old. If this infestation could stop here, with the parasite not passed on to any other children, the babies could stay with their parents. Otherwise, the Public Health Service was prepared to quarantine them. The responsible press, should it learn of this, would put a permanent lock on the quarantine ("Quarantine Only Weapon To Halt Spread Of Parasites, Doctors Say"). The irresponsible press would put everyone's lives at risk (Plague! Demon Possession! Witch Spawn! Foals of the Apocalypse!). Public reaction could be terrible; the continuing depression meant all it took to ignite riots was a suspicion of demons, witchcraft, or whatever else people could frame as scapegoats. Annabel sometimes felt she was living in the Dark Ages, but with Internet and tea bags.

Although maybe these Dark Ages had begun earlier than this century. Supposedly Annabel's first-cousin-once-removed, Paula, who had died of a fever in 1995 while doing humanitarian work in Nicaragua, had encountered something in the jungle that she had described as "a spirit of pure violence, born of human violence." And Cousin Paula had been a scientist.

The doorbell rang again.

Annabel peered through the peephole. A man stood there. She didn't recognize him, until she did. *Keith.*

Annabel undid the bolts and locks, flung open the door. They stared at each other.

The emaciated, mewling, addicted creature she had last seen in his bedroom had vanished. Keith, a year older than she, had grown taller and filled out. His skin was smooth around the little mustache, his eyes clear and bright.

"Don't look at my hair like that," Keith said, his voice thick. "There's no N-cap there. There never will be again."

"Come in," Annabel said.

He did, smelling of spring air, never taking his eyes off her. She took his jacket. They settled into the living room. Neither of them knew what to say.

When the teakettle shrilled, it got better. Annabel made them both tea and they sat at the kitchen table, as they used to do as children eating peanut butter on toast. She said, "You got clean."

"Yes. That last time, when you found me...I nearly died. If it hadn't been for you, I would have. I wanted to thank you in person. Your mother gave me your address."

"She came to the door?"

"No. I emailed her. You mean she doesn't open the door? Agoraphobia?"

Annabel nodded. He'd always been quick, much smarter than she was, and he knew her family as well as her own.

Once, nobody had known her as well as Keith had, not even Hannah.

"How did you get clean?"

"An amazing doctor. He got me into a fancy rehab place. I don't know what strings he pulled or why he thought I was worth it. After I got out, he got me to test for a new program at BU to train engineers and mathematicians. Not enough of them are getting trained, too many people are relying on magical thinking instead."

"So you're at college?"

"Not really. This program goes through BU but it's separate, funded directly by Carlos Riguerrez." Keith said this casually, but Annabel saw the pride underneath.

"Really? The software guy? Who invented the three-D holo software?"

"That's him. He's a gazillionaire and he invests in what he calls 'science of the future.'"

"Keith—you've *met* him?"

"Several times, it's part of the BU program. Riguerrez is amazing. You know that the second you meet him. The last time, he took us all down to tour the spaceport he's building in Pennsylvania."

They were talking more easily now, almost like the old days. Both cups of tea, half drunk, were growing cold.

Keith said, "What about you, Annie? You're living here with Hannah, right? Why was your mother so reluctant to give me your address until I bullied it out of her? Was it because she thinks I'm low-life scum?"

Annabel didn't want to lie to him. She had never lied to Keith, not even when he'd been lying to her. And it would be such a relief to tell somebody else the truth. But Hannah, and maybe even Paul, would kill her. So—let them! Whose life was this, anyway?

The answer to *that* was so complicated that Annabel's lip curled in derision. Keith saw it.

"What is it, Annabel? What's wrong?" He reached for her hand.

Annabel snatched it back; Paul had emphasized that even though so far she seemed to have infected only small children with skin-to-skin contact, they didn't really know. Hurt came into Keith's eyes. Annabel couldn't bear that.

"Keith—it's not what you think."

"You don't want me to touch you. I understand." He started to stand.

"No, you don't! I might be contagious!"

He paused halfway out of his chair. "Contagious with what?"

"It's kind of a long story."

"I want to hear it."

Annabel took a deep breath. But before she could begin, Keith said, "Only—have you got some coffee instead of this goddamn tea? It tastes like weeds."

No need for defenses right now. The other large organism could not be a host—far too old—but was not a danger, either. The entity knew that because none of the host's own defense hormones circulated in its body. In fact, new and different hormones had appeared, and were affecting those parts of the host connected with reproduction. The entity was cautiously interested.

"Wow," Keith said, when Annabel had finished.

"So now you run screaming into the night, right? To escape the infected and demonic woman?"

Keith grinned. "Well, it's mid-afternoon, so I guess I'll have to hang around for a while."

She put her elbows on the table, beside the drained coffee mugs, and leaned forward. "Keith, aren't you repulsed by me?"

"Were you repulsed when you found me with that N-cap?"

"Yes."

He laughed, painfully. "Well, you were right to be repulsed. But this is different. You didn't choose it. And Annabel, for whatever it's worth, I don't think these so-called parasites have really changed you. You seem just the way I remember you. Just Annabel."

Nothing he could have said would have pleased her more. She grasped his hand, his fingers strong and warm. Keith's eyes darkened. He got up, pulled her to her feet, and kissed her.

When the kisses were done, and the cuddling on Annabel's bed—they didn't go farther than that, not yet—and the murmuring in the dark, Annabel said, "Keith, will you take me someplace? Now?"

"Sure. You mean to dinner? I'm afraid I haven't got very much money but—"

"Not to dinner. Out to your old house."

"I sold it, Annie. As partial payment for rehab."

"I don't want to actually go to your house. Or mine. I want to go to that field down the block where we used to play soccer."

He raised himself on one elbow to peer at her. "Why?"

She told him, adding, "Only you can't let me try to hold any little kids we see. Okay?" With Keith, she would feel as safe as with Hannah.

"Okay. But dress warm—it's getting dark out and it's still cold when the sun goes down."

They left the apartment, holding hands, to take the train to Boston. They never got there.

In eighteen months Paul Apley had learned a lot about the parasites. The trouble was, none of it made sense.

Carbon-based organisms that nonetheless were not DNA-based could only have developed on a separate evolutionary path, sequestered from the main history of life on Earth (deep in the mountain?), and non-competitive with it. But then why was it using humans as hosts? The only other explanation that had occurred to Paul had been immediately rejected. He wasn't going to join the legions of nutcases who believed that space aliens were—pick one—(a) here to join the angels in saving humanity, (b) here to join the demons in corrupting humanity, (c) here as updated familiars for witches, or (d) here as left-overs after they built the pyramids and Stonehenge and the ruins at Chichen Itza.

On the other hand, some very respectable scientists, including Francis Crick and Stephen Hawking, had believed that both panspermia and pangenesis were possible: clouds of spores coming in from space on comets that had either started or influenced early life in the primordial seas. If so, Annabel's organisms might predate the evolutionary development of DNA. Or, these might be latecomer spores. But in either case, Annabel was an unlikely host; they wouldn't have evolved to colonize her.

There were other puzzles. Usually, hosts suffered most when a parasite—virus, bacterium, protist, worm, or fungus—first crossed over to a new species. Unadapted to the host, the parasite usually caused massive damage, destroying tissue and creating agonizingly painful inflammation. Yet Annabel was fine.

In humans, IgE antibodies fought parasites. Annabel had none.

Moreover, transmission seemed to require much more than momentary skin-to-skin contact. Not an efficient mode of spreading the infection.

Paul and his team—there were now three of them, housed in a building the CDC had equipped for them on the decaying Boston waterfront, plus Emily doing field work—had made some progress. If they didn't know why Annabel could be a host for the parasites, they knew a lot more about how. Some of the mechanisms were analogues for how known parasites operated.

Like *Schistosoma mansoni*, the parasites released chemicals that softened tough human skin, letting the organism plunge into its host.

Like *Plasmodium*, which causes malaria, it then immediately hid inside tissue, where macrophages from the immune system had more trouble finding it. Malaria hid in the liver; this organism in and on nerve cells and their myelin sheaths. Ordinarily cells would slice up their unwanted penetrators and then present pieces of DNA on the cell surface for the immune system to tailor T-cells to destroy it. But there was no DNA to present.

Also like *Plasmodium*, once outside nerve cells, this organism continued to elude the immune system by constantly changing the molecules in its outer coat. As soon as macrophages developed means to identify the invaders, the parasites became somebody else, like a truly clever spy changing identities.

Like *Trichinella*, Annabel's parasites could commandeer internal cell machinery to produce more of whatever it needed.

Like some blood flukes (although not the eggs), they didn't seem to be causing trouble in Annabel's tissues.

And so on. But what were the organisms doing in Annabel in the first place? And how could they be removed? The immune system made its own deadly toxins to attack invaders, and enough of these would kill not only them but the host. Somehow the parasites were circumventing that immune-system response, and Paul could not figure out how. Nor could he be sure that some disgruntled parents weren't breaking the voluntary isolation of their children. The oldest of them was already being home schooled, out of necessity. How long could that be enforced for twenty-three kids?

How long before the press got the story?

What if there were more than twenty-three infected kids?

April, his lab parasitologist, came through from the lab, stripping off her gloves and shaking her head. "No luck with the test."

"Damn."

"There's something else I'd like to try, but I need absolutely fresh samples from Annabel. Can you get her in here tomorrow?"

"Probably." Annabel had been less cooperative lately, which was another worry. Well, who could blame her? She was nineteen years old; she should be out drinking and partying and whatever else nineteen-year-olds did these days. Paul, forty-three, felt about a hundred. But, then, he'd never been much of a partyer.

April frowned. "She—"

His wrister rang, the dedicated sound for an emergency. Paul said, "Annabel?"

"Oh, come quick! The SLA stopped the train and came aboard! And I...I think I killed someone!"

Annabel and Keith had caught the T in Boston to the station and then a train to Framingham, where most of the commuters had gotten off. There weren't very many; the economy had somehow gotten even worse over the last few months. Something to do with a collapse in China, which had torpedoed currency in Europe and South America—Annabel didn't really understand it. The train, so old that the metal floor had been worn into slight indentations by generations of feet, continued past Framingham to the rural stops.

Then it had lurched to a halt. Keith and she were in the second car behind the engine. He said, "Did you hear that? It sounded like a gunshot!"

She had heard it. *Not again.* She, like the other six people left in the train, raised her wrister and called the cops. But this time was not like five years ago.

Three men burst through the door leading from the first car to the second. They carried guns and wore what had evolved from a shoulder patch to an entire SLA soldier uniform: lightweight body armor, belts with weapons, the confused blue emblem of wings, Buddha, and serpent. "Everybody! Off the train now! This transport is requisitioned for the holy war!"

The other six passengers scrambled out the door and into a field of wildflowers. Two of the men raced through the car and into the next one of the train. The third man stood waving his gun at Keith and Annabel. "You! Go!" His voice was deep and his beard streaked with gray. As Annabel looked into his eyes, so full of hate, something happened to her.

"Annabel, come on!" Keith pulled her in the direction of the door.

It happened fast. Rage flooded her, along with the superhuman knowledge that she could do anything, anything at all—she was invincible. She sprang forward, opened her mouth, and spat full in the "soldier's" face at the same time she punched him so hard in the neck that he went down.

Caught by surprise, he had fired but the shot went wide, ricocheting off the train walls as an echo had once ricocheted off a mountain meadow: *ME me me....*

The boy, his face smeared with a huge amount of saliva, dropped to his knees, screaming and clawing at his face. A moment later, he was dead.

Keith gaped, but only for a moment. Annabel, her brain still flooded, kicked the body at her feet. When Keith grabbed her arm, she turned on him and opened her mouth. But then she closed it again.

No. Not a second danger. And the defenses were depleted anyway.

"Annabel..."

"I'm coming," she said, and they jumped from the train and ran before any more SLA soldiers entered the car. Annabel's knees shook, but she ran with Keith until she could run no more and the train had started again and was pulling away and she could call Hannah and Paul and then collapse, sobbing, on the ground.

Hannah coached on what to say when she was arrested, but no one arrested her. There were too many others to arrest.

The train went back to Boston, picking up SLA soldiers at pre-arranged stops, and they stormed the State House with its iconic golden dome admired by generations of tourists. The state militia fought them there, but not before the advance guard, the one that arrived before the reinforcements on the train, had taken the building and killed eighteen people. One of them was the governor of Massachusetts. By the time it was over, nearly three hundred people were dead, the President had declared a state of martial law, and the United States Army occupied Boston.

"This will break the SLA power," Hannah said grimly, pacing around the apartment. "Public opinion will turn against them now."

"Don't bet on it," Emily said. She stared at Annabel with a mixture of horror and fascination.

Keith and Hannah looked at Annabel, too. Paul bent over her, taking a scraping of cells from the lining of her cheek. He really wanted an fMRI, but it was too late: Whatever event had happened in Annabel's brain was long since over. He'd have to settle for blood samples, cerebral-spinal fluid, the new Schrader-Tucker tests for detecting the aftermath of brain events in both, and accounts from Annabel and Keith.

Annabel, pale, held tight to Keith's hand—and why hadn't Paul known before now that there was a boyfriend in the picture? The kid wasn't even wearing latex gloves, for chrissake. She said, "Turn on the news."

Hannah stopped pacing. "Annabel—"

"I want to know!"

Hannah complied, and there were scenes of the attacks on trains, photographed by amateurs on their wristers or tablets, and then sharper, more detailed ones shot by dronecams at the State House. The commentary was horrified, outraged, angry.

"Those are newscasters. I want a call-in show. Get Dov Levin."

Hannah accessed the site and they watched holos of callers all telling Dov Levin the same thing: *This isn't what the Age of Imagination was supposed to be! I'm a witch/angel host/ Transcender/New Spiritualist/psychic/elf princess/regressed survivor of the Spanish Armada, and I'm peaceful and law-abiding! These so-called soldiers hijacked the truth for their own violent ends. They're throwbacks to the Age of Technology—look, they used guns!*

Hannah murmured, "'When culture and science clash, science always loses.'"

But no one was listening, and only she and Annabel were actually paying attention to the news. Keith watched Annabel. So did Emily, her face speculative and oddly predatory. Paul bagged his samples, his mind filled with questions: Had Annabel really killed someone by spitting at them? How? What had caused her neural hijacking, if that was in fact what it had been?

A few days later, he had at least partial answers.

He sat in his lab at MIT, which had taken over more room as the scope of the project grew. Now there was a clean lab for April and her assistant, an office, and an animal lab lined with mouse cages. Behind Paul the animals squeaked and burrowed. They had been useless; Todd, the animal pathologist, had so far not succeeded in infecting any of them with any of Annabel's aberrant cells. In mice, the cells just quietly died.

The scraping from Annabel's mouth revealed yet more strange cells. They were attached to dissolvable sacs holding the strongest kind of toxin that immune-system components used to attack invaders, only in far greater concentration, plus molecules that, had the membranes broken in Annabel's mouth, would have killed her. When she spit what she described as "more saliva that I thought I had," the sacs had dissolved. The toxins had hit the boy's eyes and face, first blinding him, then dripping into his open screaming mouth and killing him.

The whole episode had been triggered, as best as Paul could deduce with Schrader-Tucker tests, by brain signals which brought about massive neural firings in two parts of her brain. Chemical signals had tsunamied the amygdalae, those seats of rage and aggression. Simultaneously, dopamine had surged through Annabel's nucleus accumbens, much as if she had taken a hit of the street-drug Ecstasy. But whereas Ecstasy made you energetically dance and be joyful and love the whole world, this surge of dopamine, in conjunction with enormous floods of adrenalin, had given Annabel not only her towering and uncharacteristic rage but also the strength to knock down a grown man, akin to the frail grandmother who lifts a car off her trapped grandchild. It was possible that, if the saliva toxin had failed, she could have torn that SLA soldier apart with her bare hands.

Taken together, it was a defense system. The parasites were protecting their host.

To do that, they had controlled her behavior.

Many parasites could change their hosts' behavior, and even their metabolism. The parasitic wasp *Cotesia congregata* altered the way tobacco hookworms processed food. Another species of wasp turned cabbage worms not only into incubators for the wasps' eggs and food for the larvae, but also into bodyguards for the subsequent cocoons. Thorny-headed worms forced small crustaceans to not flee from ducks into the safe bottom of ponds, but instead to swim up to the light so that ducks could eat them. Many parasites had mastered the language of their hosts' neurotransmitters and hormones, coming up with molecules to modify those for the parasites' own uses.

But—

Given what he had just learned—or might have learned, Paul clung desperately to the uncertainty built into all hypotheses—these were not really parasites on Annabel. Parasites took and did not give. This was something else. Paul's orderly mind tested the word, rejected it, and then was forced to accept it.

Symbiote.

Annabel was now two organisms, inseparably intertwined, each benefitting the other. The organisms had cells not only in her brain but in her optic, olfactory, and auditory nerves; her thalamus, the brain's signal switchboard; her skin; deep into her limbic system. Annabel provided locomotion to reach new hosts, raw materials for nourishment, senses with which to perceive the outer world. The organism provided defense and, for all Paul knew, Annabel's perfect health, which he had assumed was merely the genetics of particularly lucky youth.

Symbiosis. Was the second partner conscious?

It was such a fantastic idea that Paul dismissed it immediately. Besides, science couldn't even agree on what caused consciousness in humans, let alone in...whatever this thing was. However, Paul knew one thing: This was too big now to be a research byway. The director of the CDC was going to have to inform the White House.

How? *"Mr. President, a teenage girl is now a symbiote with a possibly alien species, and so are twenty-three adorable pre-schoolers in Boston"*? They would think him crazy.

Maybe he was.

No. He had data, samples, hypotheses, replicable results, all the things you were supposed to have when you did science. This was not a bid for attention from some demented imagination-age delusional. It only sounded like one.

Yesterday Paul had done an uncharacteristic thing. Not much given to fancifulness, he never read fiction and seldom went to the movies. But last night he had watched three old films on his tablet: *Alien* and *The Puppetmasters* and *The Thing*. He watched them all the way through. Then, groaning, he'd had an unusual and very large belt of bourbon. Even long before the Age of Imagination, no one had been able to imagine anything like Annabel except as horror.

Emily came into the lab, carrying a stack of flimsies. She saw his face, and said, "What?"

He told her and she listened eagerly. Really eagerly, which was good because it showed she could transcend the dislike they'd always felt for each other. Paul was going to need his whole team. He had to run repeated tests on these samples; any findings he presented had to stand up to extreme scrutiny. He would face massive scientific skepticism, massive governmental preoccupation with outbreaks of SLA violence, and the usual massive machinery of bureaucracy, slow as snails. He had to be sure. Science demanded no less.

VIII

ANNABEL AND KEITH CLIMBED THE STAIRS—the elevator had broken again—to the roof of Annabel's apartment building. It was the first time Annabel had left the apartment, for her protection and everybody else's, since the aborted train trip a month ago.

The day after the attack on the State House, she and Keith had become lovers. Hannah actually seemed glad to have Keith around pretty much all the time; Annabel suspected it took some of the burden off Hannah. She was involved in the biggest case of her career, not against the SLA but against a company that stood accused of importing and selling the kind of N-caps that had nearly destroyed Keith. Hannah was junior counsel, but she was present at top-level meetings even if she didn't get to do much talking. Annabel had trouble imagining a scenario in which Hannah didn't talk much.

They emerged onto the roof. The early summer night smelled wonderful, warm air scented with the tang of salt from the harbor. Twelve stories below, Boston looked like the war zones on the news of other countries. Well, it was. Soldiers patrolled the streets, tanks stood at the ready in every neighborhood, and arrests were ongoing. The SLA had had a mole in State House security, which was how they'd initially gotten in.

"Don't look down," Keith said.

"I'm not afraid of heights."

"I meant at the soldiers."

Annabel smiled, without mirth. "That won't change the fact that I killed a man."

"Who might have killed you. It was self-defense, Annie. Anyway, you didn't really do it."

"No, my termites did."

"Don't call them that."

"That's what they are, isn't it? An infestation. A plague. Like fleas on a rat, only the fleas are inside me."

Keith didn't answer. Probably he was sick of this conversation, which they'd had over and over. Sick of her self-pity and self-loathing. Annabel was sick of it, too. All at once she seized his hand, which had also happened over and over. "I'm sorry, Keith! I'm sorry!"

"It's all right. Look up, Annabel. That's what we came for."

Annabel looked up, at the first clear night in weeks. Her breath caught in her throat. The lights of Boston dimmed the stars a little, but there were not as many lights as there used to be, and east toward the harbor, nearly none. Overhead the summer triangle, Altair and Vega and Deneb, shone brightly. Annabel gazed, and it happened again, just as it had in a field thick with snow.

Holiness. Mystery. Everything one and everything interconnected, all of it. One. And I, too, part of that vast starry expanse, and not just in a physical way... The feeling went on and on, and she was more than Annabel, she was everything.

When the feeling finally faded, Keith sat on a rotting pile of lumber, watching her.

"That's real," Annabel whispered.

"I believe you."

She sat beside him. "Paul says it's not. He says what I feel is 'a well-documented phenomenon.' He says it happens to experienced meditators, Buddhist monks and nuns who pray a lot and those types. He says—" Annabel's voice took on a savage edge "—that blood flow was redirected in my brain, toward the focus centers and away from the posterior parietal lobes, which tell me where my body ends. Less blood flow, and I feel my body dissolve, and then I focus on the stars and... presto! Annabel has a mystic experience! Paul wants to take even this away from me. But...*it is real.* It's not my termites!"

He put his arm around her.

"Keith—why aren't you afraid of me? I'm a monster."

"You're not. You're Annabel." And then, "I knew you when we used to pretend to be frogs."

This struck both of them as so ridiculous that they laughed aloud. Annabel said, "We were grubby little kids."

"Now we're grubby big kids."

"You can't ever marry me. I can't have children. I'd infect them. Wait, I'm sorry, I shouldn't say that about marriage, I don't know what I should say—" She put her head in her hands and sobbed.

Keith, not looking at her, said, "I'm going to become a space engineer."

Annabel raised her head, confused and a little affronted. "You are?"

"Yes. The private space programs are just roaring along, thanks to Carlos Riguerrez. I've already got half the credits I need for graduation because I tested out of so many courses... yay, brilliant me. In two more years I'll be qualified through this special program to work on ground crews at the new Riguerrez Spaceport, and I'll make a good salary. I'll move there, and you'll marry me, and we'll get off Earth together. We won't even need kids."

We. Space. Stars. Such a sweet feeling came over Annabel, washing her in delight, that she rose to her feet. She could have risen up into the air, floated gently like a balloon all the way to the stars. "I love you, Keith."

"And I've loved you all my life. It will be all right, Annabel. We'll make it all right."

"Yes." For that moment, anyway, she believed it.

***

Hannah sat facing Paul in his lab, where she'd never been before. She shouldn't be there now, but Paul had insisted. The lab smelled of rats in their cages along the back wall, of disinfectant, of odd chemicals. Unknown machinery whirred softly. Hannah should be at her own odorless office, preparing a critical brief in the case of *Massachusetts v. Palliter et. al.* There was fresh wire-tapping evidence that the Chinese makers of the deadly N-caps were branching out. Instead of relatively crude, electrical methods of stimulating the brain's "pleasure centers," the underground company was developing biological methods of stimulation, much harder to detect. So far the case was based on violating technology import-export laws, but if the charges could be broadened to include biologicals...

"Hannah, are you listening?"

"Of course I'm listening. You said that you wanted to talk to me without Emily or the others. Why? You said you don't have any new findings on Annabel."

"Not new findings, but a new interpretation, and I need you to hear it first. Because I'm going to have to take it more public."

She stiffened. "That would endanger Annabel!"

"It's the only way we can secure more safeguards for Annabel. I mean, federal safeguards. But first I need to tell you what I'm going to present to my director. You know, a critical element of very early evolution may have depended on symbiosis."

"Symbiosis?"

"Yes. Serial endosymbiosis theory. It says that in the very early days of life on Earth, swimmer organisms merged with heat- and sulfur-loving microbes to make a new kind of cell that incorporated both survival methods. Then later, when oxygen increased in the atmosphere, anaerobic phagocytes were added, and when you added proteobacteria to the mix, you got something very like present-day mitochondria that—"

"Paul," Hannah said with what she hoped sounded like patience, "cut to the chase."

Paul rushed on. "All life on Earth started by organisms merging into each other. That's how you got new species before Darwinian evolution began to separate them again. Your brain has microtubules in its nerve cells that are exactly like the microtubules in bacteria. Your gut is full of symbiotic bacteria that you can't live without, and they can't live without you. The mitochondria in your cells are the descendants of free-living bacteria, captured by a larger organism that was your ancestor. The cilia lining your throat match the DNA of archaebacteria. You exist as a mass of incorporated organisms."

Hannah said, ominously quiet, "But it's not my gut or throat or brain we're talking about, is it? It's Annabel's."

"Yes. Of course. The organisms in her are a part of her now. They're not parasites, they're symbiotes. We know that in the past attackers became symbiotes and, over time, became organelles in the human body. That's what Annabel may have. The parasites conferred on her the evolutionary advantage of a novel defense system, however little we might like that. They may be working to confer on her other advantages. We don't know. But she is now Annabel plus. And, Hannah, that's not all bad! Long ago parasites caused the first appearance of a human immune system. Parasites may have also caused the evolution of human sex. In fact, a human fetus is a sort of parasite. All evolution is inevitable, it proceeds along its own path and—"

Hannah stood. "It's a good thing you're not a lawyer, Paul. You have no idea how to present a case. You're telling me that my sister is now some sort of alien being?"

"No, that's what I'm *not* telling you! She's Annabel. But she's also more than Annabel, possibly the next step in human evolution. Or a false step, a branch that won't last, we just don't know. But these organisms can take over her brain when they need to, can activate the defense system, and—more!—can influence what substances like dopamine exist, and in what concentration, in what part of her brain. They can—"

"Dopamine?" Hannah said sharply. "You mean, like N-caps do? Are you saying my sister has inside her the equivalent of an *N-cap*?"

"No, no....it's not the same. But that's the whole point, Hannah, we don't know what these organisms can, or will, do. In Annabel or in the other children, when their symbiotes mature enough. Or maybe they have already. Annabel needs to be at the CDC or NIH, she needs to be studied—"

"Like a lab rat!"

"—and, more important, protected."

"I'm not letting you take her."

"I can get a court order. You know that. Now, more easily than ever."

He could. Maybe he should. No, this was Annabel, who'd already tried so hard to comply with science, who'd stayed at home, bored and out of the work force, for over a year, who'd given everything—

The lab door burst open and April rushed in. Paul turned on her. "I said not to interrupt us!"

"I'm sorry but I had to. Keith Brywood just called me when he couldn't reach you. Why did you block the lab communications? It's Annabel...she's gone! They took her!"

Hannah seized April's wrist. "Took her? Who?"

"Keith doesn't know! He's in the hospital, they hit him hard and he just now came to—he called right away!"

For the first and last time in his life, a hunch came over Paul, a completely unbidden, uncultivated, coming-from-somewhere-else feeling. Later he would analyze this until he'd made it rational: he'd had all the data before, his mind had finally put it together, it was the creative unconscious working in the same way that scientists and novelists "got ideas" when they weren't looking for them. But right now, it felt like knowledge delivered to him by some supernatural force.

He said, "Where's Emily?"

They had violated Annabel's isolation strictures and gone to the waterfront. Near pier four, a carnival had been set up, a tawdry traveling affair quick to take advantage of the lifting of martial law since the SLA had gone so quiet. Annabel and Keith didn't care that the carnival was tawdry. Giddy with the shiny new declaration of love and their richly imagined future, they felt invulnerable. They were going to be together forever. They were going to marry and go live at Riguerrez spaceport in Pennsylvania. They were going, someday, to go to space. Right now, they were going to go to the carnival.

They bought greasy French fries, rode on the Ferris wheel, threw rubber rings at bottles and won a cheap stuffed dolphin with a vaguely malevolent grin. Annabel hung onto Keith's arm and felt happier than she could remember. Her termites were almost forgotten. She was merged not with them but with Keith, and every time she looked into his eyes, she felt she was drowning in their beloved depths.

"Tired, Annie?"

"A little." It was nearly midnight and the carnival was closing down, locking up rides and booths, turning off lights. The air had turned cooler. Arms around each other's waists, Annabel and Keith started toward the nearest T station.

The black van barreled along the street and jolted to a stop. Men jumped from the back. Keith had no time to fight, nor Annabel to spit. They hit him with something hard; they clamped an evil-smelling cloth over her mouth and nose. The drug took almost instant effect. She was thrown into the back of the van, and as it sped away, the world went dark.

No time to react, and no response from the host!

Annabel woke tied to a bed. Her mouth was bound with duct tape. The entire small room, which held nothing except the bed, rocked rhythmically. Dim light came from a recessed overhead fluorescent, and an old-fashioned keypad was wired to the door.

A boat. She was on some sort of boat. That round window high on the opposite wall was a porthole, painted black. Were they—oh god, no—out on the ocean somewhere?

Keith. He had cried out, and she hadn't seen what happened then alongside the van. Was he dead?

She lay there for a long time, or what seemed a long time, consumed by dread. Nothing happened, but she decided that the boat wasn't moving; the rocking was too even, like being buffeted at anchor or something (she had seldom been on boats), instead of the pitch and roll of real waves. So was she still in Boston? How long had she been knocked out? *Was Keith dead?*

The cabin door opened. A person entered, the last kind of person Annabel had expected to see: an old woman, hunched over, dressed in some fantastic cross between a sari and a Halloween costume. Rich patterned silk draped the bent old body, ending at bare feet yellowed and studded with calluses. Around her wrinkled neck hung a thin chain dangling a cross, a pentacle, and a yin/yang circle. Gray hair straggled from a medieval gable hood, like ladies wore in Tudor England, its black veil of coarsely woven cotton. She carried a big wicker basket.

Her accent was pure South Boston, incongruous with a bastardized and intermittent version of Shakespearean English. "Awake, I see. Prithee, how be you?"

Annabel couldn't speak for the duct tape, but she glared.

"I be Mother Moran," the woman said, not without dignity. "They tell me you be not a believer."

In what?

"Some souls be stubborn, verily. You shall learn, or the universe shall teach you. You smell bad—okay, let us get you bathed."

Annabel had just wet herself. She'd done it deliberately, aware of the fullness of her bladder, hoping to lure the old woman closer. If her termites would react as they had in the train, flooding her with strength enough to break her ropes...

They didn't. Annabel lay helpless as the old woman, with surprising deftness, cut off her jeans and underpants, then turned her this way and that to strip off the sheet and to wash her with soap and a bottle of warm water from the basket. She put a clean sheet on the bed and another over Annabel, now naked from the waist down. Annabel could not work herself free, nor summon any superhuman strength. The old woman was not arousing enough fear.

She was a talker. "Aye, soon enough the universe will teach you the necessity of belief. The old ways be dead, you know, and a pox upon them. Science, the false god, brought us to this sorry state. Belief in the old ways, in the Great Unseen, shall restore us. All through history the Old Souls have glimpsed part of it, and were burnt or hung or drowned for their wisdom. But now imagination shall be the path to the Great Unseen, and the good times shall come to the Earth, with the Way and the Path a shining light beckoning us all to enlightenment."

She finished with both Annabel and her prayerful mish-mash, gave Annabel a smile of surprising sweetness, and repacked her basket. Her sari-draped body hid the keypad from Annabel as she tapped in the code to open the door.

Alone again, Annabel struggled against her bonds. Nothing. If she were Hannah or Keith or her father, someone resourceful, maybe she could have figured out a way to escape. But she was only Annabel, stupid and ineffective, infested with equally ineffective termites.

But the boat's slight rocking didn't change. At least they had not yet left for wherever they (*who?*) were taking her.

It wasn't much, but it was all she had.

"Where is Emily?" Paul said.

April, the most focused and steady lab pathologist Paul had ever seen, tended to scatteredness outside the lab. She flapped her free hand pointlessly and said, "Emily?"

Hannah still held April's other wrist. Paul could see Hannah forcing calm on herself. She said, "Call Keith back on your wrister. His won't work inside Mass General but yours has whatever hospital number he called from."

April called, setting the wrister on loudspeaker. A man answered: "Yes?"

Hannah said, "Keith Brywood, please."

"Who is calling?"

"This is Mr. Brywood's lawyer. To whom am I speaking?"

"Special Agent David Goldberg, FBI. What is your name, please?"

"Hannah Sevley. Please let me speak to my client."

"They took him down to X-ray. Were you with your sister and Mr. Brywood last night, Ms. Sevley?"

"I was not. I'm leaving for Mass General right now and will be there in twenty minutes. No additional conversation with my client until I arrive, Agent Goldberg."

"Got it." He broke the link.

April said, "Why can't Keith talk to the FBI? He's not a suspect!"

"Of course he is. He was the last person to see her." But then Hannah's composure broke and her face trembled. April, quick to compassion, put a sympathetic arm around Hannah, who shrugged it off and said, "I'm going now. Paul, are you coming?"

"Yes. But, April—where's Emily?"

Hannah finally caught it. She said sharply, "Why do you want Emily? What does she know?"

He didn't answer, not having anything rational to say. But something must have shown on his face because Hannah said even more sharply, "What has Emily done?"

"I don't know. Probably nothing. I don't have any reason to—April, has she been in this morning?"

"I haven't seen her."

"Has Todd?"

"This is Todd's day off."

Paul raised his wrister and called Emily. No one answered. He left a message to call him back immediately. To April he said, "Find Emily and tell her to call me. Call her every five minutes until you get her. If you can't, go to her apartment."

"All right," April said, looking scared.

Racing together out of the building to catch a cab, Hannah said, "What do you suspect about Emily? Tell me, Paul."

Hannah was a lawyer. She could injure Emily, could perhaps bring legal actions that Paul only vaguely understood, and he didn't really have anything to go on. But Hannah was also Annabel's sister. He weighed truth against compassion and compromised. "I don't have any reason to suspect Emily of anything. But she's been jumpy the last few days, and…and that's it."

"I don't believe you."

"That's all I have, Hannah." Except that Emily disliked Annabel and, more profoundly, disapproved of her. Annabel, idle (although through no fault of her own!), supported by her sister, pretty and appealing and uneducated. Whereas Emily, intelligent and plain and fiercely ambitious, worked like a slave for the paltry salary of a post-doc in a culture that now publicly scorned science. But that didn't mean that Emily was guilty of anything more than bitterness mixed with envy.

Nonetheless, the irrational feeling wouldn't leave him.

At the hospital, Keith was not yet back from X-ray. Agent Goldberg began to question Hannah about Annabel's routine, movements, contacts, Internet activity, finances. "Do you know of any circumstances that might give someone a reason to abduct Annabel?"

And Hannah hesitated.

Agent Goldberg's gaze sharpened.

This was it, then. They were going public, or at least going beyond the CDC, and this wasn't the way it was supposed to happen. Paul was supposed to have the Director with him, and CDC lawyers, and graphs and lab results and an orchestrated press conference. This wasn't the way it was supposed to happen.

Hannah said, "This is Dr. Paul Apley, Annabel's physician. She has a condition that may or may not have bearing on finding her. Dr. Apley will explain."

"Annabel," Paul began. "Annabel—" *is a symbiote, possibly the next step in human evolution, who could kill you with her spit, lift a car off you in her rage, produce surges of dopamine in her brain that would keep her giggling with pleasure without the aid of street drugs or N-caps or—*

The realization of what Emily had done, and why, lit his mind like a solar flare. Instantly he rejected it. She was a *scientist*, for chrissake, that meant something—

Half the spies who had betrayed the United States had been intelligence agents. Half the dirty arms dealers had been Army weapons experts. Half the talent working on deadly bioweapons in Asia or the Middle East had been trained in the United States, and all of them were scientists. He was naïve, and knew he was naïve, and Annabel's life might be at stake. Although if he was right, they would certainly not kill her.

"Dr. Apley?" Goldberg said sharply.

Paul said, "Annabel has a medically exploitable condition. I'll explain to you what it is and how I think that N-cap makers could use it. But first I think you should alert your colleagues—the law enforcement agencies, I mean—to search for Dr. Emily Jane Zimmer."

The host was in a state of anxiety but didn't seem in immediate danger. The molecules associated with acute fear were not circulating in the host's body. The entity didn't understand why the host was restrained, but the restraints in no way threatened its own functioning, so it did nothing. Its energies served its own life processes, its continuing evolution, and the constant maneuvers to outwit the host's immune system.

More hosts would be welcome. But no babies, with their undeveloped and very plastic neural systems, had come along in a long time.

Meanwhile, the organism dissolved certain vesicles on the edges of synapses in Annabel's brain. Serotonin molecules were released, to be taken up by receptors on the cells across her synapses. The entity added certain natural endorphins. That would help keep the host happy.

***

Annabel felt calmer, more focused. The boat had not, as far as she could tell, moved yet. When the old woman returned, carrying her enormous basket, Annabel twisted her fingers to point to her mouth and moved her jaw to indicate hunger.

"Aye, you be hungry," the woman said, in her ridiculous fake-archaic speech. If she started using "thee" and "thou," Annabel was going to seriously lose it.

From the basket the woman removed a sort of clear globe that looked like a fishbowl with a huge hole cut out of the back. She put this on her head, while Annabel stared in shock.

Her abductors knew she could spit toxins.

The only people who knew that were Hannah, Keith, Paul, and his team. Had they tortured Keith until he told? Fear and rage gripped her then, but weirdly muted, as if she somehow could only get so angry, no more. Although maybe that was a good thing. She needed to question this old horror and learn what she could.

The woman took a bottle of water and a lidded bowl from her basket. When she removed the lid, the aroma of curry widened Annabel's nostrils.

"Now sit up, my dear, as much as you can. That's it, just wiggle against the bed a bit, and I'll adjust your pillows. There. Now, I'll take off this tape, but no tricks, now. Wouldn't do you any good if you tried."

She ripped the duct tape from Annabel's mouth. It hurt but she didn't cry out. The old woman produced a spoon and began to feed her.

Annabel swallowed—the curry was delicious—and said, "Why wouldn't any 'tricks' do me any good?" If the cabin was under surveillance, she wanted to know. She didn't see any cameras, but that meant nothing.

The woman cackled, "Oh, you do be ignorant, don't you, dear? I be Mother Moran. I've got spells and charms girding this whole boat. Ones proven effective, too, or else why would they have me in charge of you?"

Annabel swallowed another mouthful. "Spells and charms? You can do that?"

"I can. I have, for all my lifetimes."

"So you work for the SLA?" *Is that who has me?*

"I work for the Great Unseen, my dear. The SLA is but a means to bring about universal enlightenment, though most of them cannot yet see that. Thinking of only their immediate aims, as be you. But Mother Moran sees much farther than that, and the best part of their imagination knows it. They would not go forward without my blessing, and they dasn't disobey me. They know how dangerous that would be."

Annabel tried to sort this out, even as she said, "Go forward where? Where are they taking me?"

"Toward enlightenment. Do you want some water?"

Annabel drank, the woman holding the water bottle. Up close, her eyes looked filmy. How well did she see? Her skin was light brown; she might have been part Black, or Arab, or Indian. Darker brown spots dotted the crevasses of her wrinkles. One lower front tooth was missing on the left side.

Kindness shone in the rheumy eyes. This was not a bad person, nor did she even seem mentally ill like the homeless who walked around Boston talking to themselves or ranting at passers-by. Mother Moran merely believed, with every brain cell she had, that she was a powerful sorceress. What had happened to her over her life? Had it been so disappointing that she had, at some point, decided to imagine a different version of herself, and then believed in it? And was that so different from more conventional religions?

Was it so different from Annabel, believing that she had somehow transcended herself—twice now—as she looked up at stars? Because that transcendence had not been her termites, it had *not*—

"What does the SLA want with me?"

"Money," Mother Moran said, succinctly and unexpectedly.

"How? Ransom?"

"I don't know. It is not my concern, my dear—that be for lesser souls to arrange. My trust be to safeguard this ship, and you."

"The ship has spells and charms on it?"

"Of course."

"Where are we going?" Annabel didn't really expect an answer, but she got one. Evidently enlightenment required truth.

"To the big ship first, and then east, where all enlightenment began."

"How far east? India? China?"

"Eat, child. Eat."

Annabel ate. But as Mother Moran packed up her basket and pulled out a roll of duct tape, Annabel tried one more question. "Why haven't we left yet? Aren't the signs right or something?"

The old face broke into a smile. "See—you begin already to learn. No, the signs be not right. Also, we wait for him to arrive from California."

"Him? Him who?"

But Mother Moran retaped Annabel's mouth, picked up her basket, and left.

To the big ship first. Boston Harbor had small boats coming and going all the time. Hannah, when she had been working on a smuggling case, had told her that although the Harbor Master had filings of which boats held berths in the various marinas, it was impossible to know who was on what boat or what was carried in and out by sea. The Coast Guard did spot inspections of papers, but organized crime always had the right papers. No one would know that this boat held a bound girl in a small locked room somewhere below deck.

But these people had learned about her before the attack. Which meant that Keith hadn't been tortured for information. So how had the SLA learned about her?

Annabel had no answer, and anyway the answer to that question wasn't what she needed. She needed to get out of here. Mother Moran was her only hope. But that crazy old woman wasn't going to help; her beliefs were all focused in another direction. Annabel had nobody but herself to rely on.

No. Not only herself. Her termites were using her. Could she maybe use them, as well? In some way besides spitting and getting furious?

That would be only fair, wouldn't it?

Clearly, FBI Special Agent Goldberg thought they were both crazy. Hannah, a lawyer, and Paul, a CDC researcher, and he believed neither of them. Ordinarily this would have filled Hannah with indignation, but she was too fearful about Annabel for it to penetrate. If that bitch Emily had betrayed Annabel to the SLA for *money*—

And Hannah had to make the call to their mother.

Having no patience with her mother's self-indulgent hiding out, Hannah had not seen her in well over a year. But Julia had a right to know that her daughter was in danger. All at once there came to Hannah the image of her mother, fingers bleeding from tearing at unyielding rock, singing to tiny Annabel trapped in the crevasse. Singing and singing until her throat was too hoarse to bring out another note...

"I have to call my mother," she said.

"What's her address?" Agent Goldberg said. "When do you think she last saw Annabel?"

"I have no idea."

He listened in on the call, for which Hannah turned her back to both him and Paul. They didn't need to see her face. "Mother? It's Hannah."

"Hannah! How are you?" And then, "What's wrong?"

"It's Annabel. She's...missing."

Julia's voice tautened. "What do you mean, 'missing'?"

"She was kidnapped. Last night. The FBI is on the case. They'll find her, they're very good at—"

"Why would anybody kidnap Annabel? She doesn't have any money! Or...is this some kind of sex thing?"

"No, no, Mom, nothing like that. The FBI thinks Annabel isn't going to be hurt or touched. It's more a …well, it's complicated."

Julia said, "Where are you? I'll catch the next train."

Paul talked to the FBI agent, who became two agents, and then four. The agents called the CDC Director through encrypted satellites. Keith was returned from X-ray, allowed to talk to Paul and Hannah and Goldberg for a few minutes, and then sequestered by his nurses. The whole circus moved to the Boston field office. An FBI medical expert arrived there and Paul had to begin his story all over again. It was clear the woman didn't believe him.

Annabel's mother arrived, terrified and bewildered. Agents interviewed her, and then she was taken away by Hannah.

More phone calls. Paul explained over and over the large number of things he had no answer to, including: the origin of the microbes that had turned Annabel into a symbiote; whether the other infected children would become like Annabel; how the parasites could be carbon-based but have a genetic system different from DNA; why they were here; why no one besides Keith, a twenty-year-old ex-addict, had ever witnessed the alleged spitting in which alleged toxins had allegedly killed a man. "Don't you understand—these are things we were researching!" he said in frustration, at which point they began asking him the same questions yet again.

However, they wouldn't answer *his* questions. Not until he said to Agent Goldberg, "Have you found Emily? For questioning?"

He said, "She left the country yesterday on a plane to Greece."

Greece. The new home for terrorists, criminals hiding out, illegal weapons development, and borderline banking houses. Ever since its economy had collapsed into total chaos, Greece had been the new destination of choice for those who wished to not be found. The government, the most corrupt in Europe, cooperated, if sufficiently bribed. Greece, once the cradle of Western civilization.

He said, "Do we have extradition treaties with Greece?"

Agent Goldberg snorted.

Another man approached Paul. "Dr. Apley, I'm Dr. Fuentes from the National Security Agency. I'd like to talk to you about why the CDC was not monitoring and quarantining these plague carriers."

"We were. And it's not a plague."

"And you think it has some actual monetary potential to an organization as anti-science as the SLA?" Fuentes's eyebrows had raised so high they threatened his hairline.

"Potentially, yes."

"Tell me about that."

Paul began yet again.

Lying on her bed in the claustrophobic cabin of the rocking boat, Annabel started by visualizing Mother Moran.

She tried to get a picture in her mind as complete as possible: the sari, the medieval headdress, the jewelry from three different belief systems, the wrinkled and liver-spotted brown face. Then she tried to hold that picture, and only that picture, in her mind. It was difficult and exhausting. An old joke of Keith's from when they were kids came to her mind: *Try not to think about a pink elephant.* She'd forgotten the punch line, but she remembered vividly that all she had been able to think of was pink elephants.

Could her termites see what she imagined? Maybe not, but she kept on, adding memories of how Mother Moran smelled and talked. She remembered Paul's term for the part of her brain that focused attention: *My cortex should be smoking by now.*

Nothing happened. Her stupid termites didn't know what she meant.

Okay, focus on rage. When she'd been in danger before, she'd suddenly been strong enough to knock down a grown man. So become furious, focus on killing Mother Moran....

Annabel knew she couldn't do it, not unless the demented old woman was holding a gun and about to fire. A spell wouldn't do it. Annabel just didn't have enough belief in spells.

All right, now what?

Put her body in danger. That's what the termites cared about.

She began to strain so hard against her bonds that the skin chafed, and then bled. She wriggled her body to the almost-sitting-up position in which Mother Moran had fed her, and banged her head hard against the headboard. The more she banged, the more pain she inflicted on herself, the angrier she got—at the termites. They were the reason she was in this condition! They were the ones that had wrecked her life and injured Keith and gotten her kidnapped!

Fury mounted in her, and blood stained the sheets.

The host was destroying itself!

The entity raced to flood it with pleasure monoamines, so that it would stop. If necessary, it could knock out the host to make it halt its dangerous, counter-productive behavior. The organism raced to release the necessary toxin from the thick-membraned sacs where they were stored—but then it halted.

The host was trying to communicate.

Instructions coded into the entity's equivalent of DNA, dormant until this perception occurred, were activated. Chemical and electrical signals raced among the web of cells, by now fully half as numerous as Annabel's neural network, and just as complex. This, the entity now understood, was why it had been sent from home. Communication must occur, and all the networking necessary to interpret Annabel's intent was present. Years of monitoring optical, cortical, hippocampal, parietal, and all the other nerves of Annabel's brain had prepared the entity for this. It did not "see" what Annabel thought, any more than a computer "sees" the program put into it. But it could draw conclusions, however untested, from Annabel's actions, the firing pattern of her neurons, and the chemicals produced by her body.

The host no longer wished to lie on this particular surface with these particular bracelets on its appendages.

The entity washed dopamine through Annabel's nucleus accumbens, While she was still giggling, it oozed acids, safely packaged into the same thick membranous sacs as the toxins in her saliva, through microtubules in her skin. The sacs emerged from her wrists, interacted with oxygen in the air, and dissolved. The acids ate slowly through the ropes.

Ten minutes later Annabel's brain had been cleansed of its ecstatic stimulant and her limbs were free.

Paul took a phone call from April, and everything got worse.

He was sitting helplessly with Hannah and her mother in Hannah's apartment, an hour after Paul had finally been released by the FBI. "Don't talk to anyone and don't leave the city," Agent Goldberg had said, surely the most unnecessary piece of advice in Fibbie history. Hannah had asked Paul to help her get her mother to Hannah's apartment, a request that Paul hadn't understood at all, until he did.

Both Hannah and Annabel were vivid and courageous women, in their different ways, but Julia Sevley seemed so tentative, so fearful, in everything she said or did that it was incredible she had given birth to these daughters. Of course, Julia was terrified for Annabel. But she seemed equally terrified of Paul, of the cab driver, of the poodle being brought up in the elevator after a walk with its owner, of Hannah's apartment, of Hannah herself. *A limp rag*, Paul thought, and knew he was being uncharitable, and didn't care. Hannah had heated something nearly indigestible for dinner, which none of them ate. Paul had run out of explanations, reassurances, and hope to offer Julia, who got on his nerves. He was exhausted. He wanted to go home.

"Well," he said, "I think I'll just—" His wrister rang. April.

"Paul, I'm still at the lab," April said. "The secure computer just delivered a time-delayed message to you. From Emily."

"Open it," he said thickly, while Hannah's face swiveled to gaze at his.

"I can't," April said, "I don't have your override password to bypass the retina scan. And it won't let me forward it to your wrister."

Emily had always been good with software. Paul said, "My password is louispasteuryougoguy, all small case. Open the message and read it aloud." After a second's hesitation, he put the wrister on loudspeaker.

Emily's face, taut-jawed and defiant, appeared on the tiny screen. "Paul. I'm sorry. This is not what was supposed to happen. I went to the press about Annabel for the public good. She's a menace to everybody—I went for the public good!"

Hannah said, "They must have paid the bitch for her story. Hugely."

"But," Emily said, and here her voice grew rich with self-justification, "I didn't know that the reporter would blab to somebody even before he'd finished marshaling his facts, or that the somebody would know an SLA soldier—but however it happened, I didn't intend any harm to Annabel or you. I just did what I thought was right. And now they'll punish me for it, so I'm leaving before anyone can do that. We don't all have rich relatives willing to support us in a life of leisure."

Hannah snorted.

"I won't be back," Emily finished defiantly. "Not that you really care one way or the other. Bye."

"Oh, she'll be back," Hannah said. "In cuffs."

Julia started to cry.

Paul raised his wrister to call Agent Goldberg.

Drops of the acid eating away at the ropes touched her wrist. Annabel's skin burned and she cried out in pain. But when the ropes fell away, she could only stare.

Did the termites do that?

Did I do that?

Did struggling so hard to get free make her parasites aware of what she herself wanted? Was that possible?

The door opened. Quickly Annabel pulled the top sheet over the severed ropes, the blood, her naked genitalia. Mother Moran came in with her everlasting basket.

"Dinner, my dear. Just let me get my helmet on, the boys out there lack the complete faith that the Great Unseen says will protect us against—"

Annabel was out of bed and on her. Before Mother Moran could reach for any kind of panic button or hidden alarm, Annabel had her on the floor, arms pinned out to the sides. The gable-shaped headdress fell off, exposing sparse gray hair. The old body was light and insubstantial, as if her bones floated, fragile straws, in a sac mostly made of wind. Annabel's head began to throb. Mother Moran closed her eyes and began to chant.

For just a moment Annabel feared that maybe the chants were real, and the Great Unseen would come to Mother Moran's aid, or a guardian angel or demon or whatever would materialize….The moment passed. Annabel caught both of the old woman's wrists in one hand and yanked the totemic mish-mash of jewelry off her neck. Of course, the panic button could be elsewhere on her clothing.

Now what?

"…and protect us from all evil, lift us into the hand of safety…."

Annabel couldn't kill her. She just couldn't. There must be another way.

Mother Moran's chanting changed to another language, Latin or Gaelic or Sanskrit or something. At the same moment, Annabel thought of her own mother. The image came clear and bright into her mind: Julia as she had been when Annabel was a child, holding Annabel by the hand, smiling down at her. They had been walking to the movies, both of them laughing at something forgotten that a six-year-old would consider funny. Red maple leaves had swirled across their feet, the air had smelled of wood smoke, and Mommy had worn a jacket as red as the leaves.

"I'm not going to hurt you," Annabel panted at Mother Moran—the headache was growing worse—"but I have to do this."

With her free hand she fished around in the big basket for duct tape. She taped Mother Moran's mouth, wrists, and ankles. Then she stripped off the old woman's sari. Underneath, Mother Moran wore a saggy bra and white, elastic-waisted underpants that somehow hurt Annabel's heart.

She lifted Mother Moran onto the bed, covered her with the sheet, and tied one wrist to the bedframe as gently as possible. Clumsily she draped the sari over herself, arranging it to cover as much as possible of her tee, hiding the nakedness of her bottom half. The sari gave off the musty smell of old flesh.

Okay, termites. You're on.

Quietly Annabel stood beside the bed and concentrated. Every few minutes she thought, *This is insane.* Then she brought her mind back to the picture in front of it, her fingers moving over her face and Mother Moran's, back again, then again. She closed her eyes so as not to see the fury in the old woman's, and then opened them again. Maybe the termites needed to see Mother Moran. Who knew what they needed?

This is insane.

Fingers moving over one face and then the other, pulling her own skin down, ignoring the sudden flashes of joy or anger or calm or alertness that came and went in her mind. Those weren't her. But they meant the termites were trying, or at least that's what she hoped it meant.

This is insane—

She felt the change begin.

The host was communicating instructions. The entity didn't understand them, but that wasn't its concern. Nor was obedience. The host's concern was self-preservation, and everything the entity sensed, in its exquisitely fine-tuned response to the host's body, said that these instructions were necessary for both of their survival. The host understood survival in the larger world better than did the entity. At long last, it was behaving as it should, for both their benefit.

The host's body naturally made melatonin. It was not hard to induce the host to make more on the top one-tenth of the host's skin, and to make it uneven in pigmentation.

The host's body also naturally made collagen, which plumped out the contours of that same one-tenth to make them firm and smooth. It was not hard to destroy some of that collagen, making the skin sag, and have some created in other areas, forming lumps.

The host's body had hair follicles all over it; hair fibers were hastily pumped out on the host's lip and chin.

All this took several hours and consumed much energy. But the host bore it patiently. From this, the entity knew the changes must be critical.

It worked as fast as it could.

Hannah said, "Here it comes."

Paul, who had not gone home after all, looked at the holo software on Hannah's laptop. He had just ended a long conference call to the CDC Director, legal counsel, and PR chief. FBI reinforcements were on their way, to both here and MIT.

"CDC HIDING PLAGUE IN BOSTON!" screamed a very agitated news avatar. "COVER-UP DECADES OLD—PUTTING YOUR CHILDREN AT RISK!"

Paul knew he should watch ("Know your enemy"), but all at once he could not. He'd reached the end of his ability to cope. Julia had gone into Hannah's bedroom and the cops had cordoned off Annabel's room and told them not to disturb anything in there. So Paul went into the bathroom, the only room left, and closed the door. He sat on the toilet, head bowed, and wondered how bad it was going to get.

He suspected very, very bad.

Annabel peered at herself in the back of the shiny metal spoon with which Mother Moran had been going to feed her more curry, and she gasped. The spoon wasn't a very good mirror, giving her a reflection that was too long and too narrow. But it was clear enough for her to see her splotchy brown skin, her sags and lumps and wrinkles, her chin hairs.

But I'm only nineteen!

Dumb, dumb. If the termites could do this, then they could just put it all back later. She hoped.

Hastily, light-headed and ferociously hungry but needing to move after the long hours of motionlessness, Annabel put on Mother Moran's gable-shaped headdress. Her hair had not turned gray, not even at the roots; she pulled out a few strands and examined them, just to be sure. Evidently the termites couldn't do that. Annabel adjusted the headdress and its veil to hide every bit of her hair. Around her neck she put the chain with its three conflicting spiritual symbols. Slowly she walked around the room, practicing both a hunched back and a shuffling gait that kept the sari draped over her pink, very young-looking toes.

When she felt ready, she turned to the door, and realized she'd forgotten that it was coded to a keypad password she didn't know.

Hannah sat numbly watching the Internet, which had been set to cycle through twenty different news sites of all types, thirty seconds on each. She didn't even try to argue in her mind with the misstatements and hysteria and demagoguery. Even the responsible news sites were in fear mode, branding the CDC as criminally negligent and Annabel as a latter-day Typhoid Mary. On the specialized news sites she was called a demon, the Anti-Christ, a child-killing witch, a mutant, an unnatural monster, the tool of a plot to destroy the United States, one of the four Horsemen of the Apocalypse, a bioweapon, and an agent of scientific fascism.

Annabel had been safer in that mountain crevasse, all those years ago.

The federal government promised to throw a quarantine around the entire city of Boston. Meanwhile, sirens sounded in the street outside. Hannah went to the window. Cop cars screeched to a halt; Agent Goldberg and five other people got out of a dark unmarked car. The press would be only minutes behind.

Hannah's stomach twisted, but she was not going to give way to terror or unhelpful anger. She was going to stay strong, for Annabel. She was not going to be Julia, cowering in the bedroom.

"Paul?" Hannah said in the direction of the bathroom. "Paul? Are you coming out of there?"

Annabel scowled at the keypad. She had come this far; she wasn't going to be stopped now. Although, really, how far had she come? She was still trapped in a boat cabin with a crazy old woman who, incredibly, was now snoring loudly on the blood-smeared bed. Well, old people needed to sleep.

"Termites," she said softly, "now what?" They had made her into an old woman; they could damn well make her into a free one.

Annabel visualized the keypad. Mother Moran touching it. Annabel touching it. Over and over.

Nothing.

Well, of course not. They couldn't read her mind. Before, she'd had to pantomime what she'd wanted them to do. They understood her through motion, emotion, nerves doing something physical. She reached out to touch the keypad, then yanked on the doorknob. Over and over.

But how could the termites know the keycode, if Annabel hadn't ever seen Mother Moran enter it? If Annabel had to wake up the old woman, threaten to hurt her in order to get the code, even actually hurt her—no, that wasn't possible. Not an old woman, batshit crazy. And if Annabel made herself get into a rage so her termites took over... But that wouldn't work either. She'd tried it. A phrase from Hannah's legalese floated into Annabel's mind: *a clear and present danger*. There had to be a clear and present danger in order for the termites to do that neural-hijacking thing. *They* had to feel threatened.

So how was she going to get out of this room, before someone came to see why Mother Moran wasn't creeping around the ship setting spells or leading a Black Mass or whatever she did?

Annabel stared hopelessly at the keyboard. To have come this far…. Her hand moved toward the keypad, almost of its own volition. She jerked it back because the feeling was so creepy. But then she gave in, and her hand touched every single key, one after the other.

The termites still didn't understand! She didn't need every key, she just needed the ones comprising the code. Stupid termites!

Annabel's hand fell to her side. Some of the keys began to glow. How….

Then she understood.

Those were the keys that Mother Moran had touched. The old woman's fingers had left sweat or oil or skin molecules or something on just those keys, and now Annabel's fingers had deposited something on top of that and the two were interacting. But in what order had Mother Moran touched them? The S and L keys shone Day-Glo orange, A, E, U, and R lighter orange. So maybe use S and L more than once…

SLA RULES.

Cheesy! Annabel touched the letters in order, and the door clicked softly. She picked up Mother Moran's basket and, head down and back hunched, left the cabin. A short metal corridor, and in the shine of a fanlight over the cabin door stood a guard, a big man in full SLA uniform. In her crouching posture, she could see his boots, chest, hands with thick fingers like bunches of bananas. And his gun.

"I ask your blessing, Mother," he said.

Paul had left, under police escort, to go home. Hannah braced herself and went into her bedroom. With any luck, Julia would be asleep. Hannah could get her night things and an extra blanket and sleep on the sofa. But if Julia was awake and fell into stupid hysterics, Hannah wasn't going to put up with it. She didn't have Annabel's patience with their mother's cowardice. Let her be asleep—

Julia wasn't. Nor was she crying. She was kneeling before Hannah's night stand, which had been cleared of its usual clutter of notes, tissues, books, and used coffee mugs. The night stand now held the bowl of flowers that Annabel placed regularly on Hannah's dresser and which Hannah barely noticed before they were dead. Beside the flowers sat a framed picture of Annabel as a young child, which Julia must have brought with her, and a small religious statue.

Hannah exploded. "Oh, fuck! You, too? Isn't it bad enough that all this irrational hocus-pocus is why Annabel's gone missing in the first place? Have you been wasting all this time praying? What the fuck is *wrong* with you!"

Julia didn't crumple. She stood and gazed steadily at Hannah. Her voice was surprisingly strong. "You think you have all the answers, Hannah, but you don't. You're brilliant and hard-working and accomplished, but you don't know everything. Here's something you don't know: In scientific studies run by universities, remote prayer has had a beneficial effect on dying patients. They live longer and show fewer symptoms. It's true. You can check it on the Internet. As I'm sure you will."

"The data—"

"Is solid and peer-juried. One of the studies, published just last year, was done at Harvard. Go ahead, Hannah, be the lawyer that you are. That I'm proud of you for being. Look it up now."

"I will!" Hannah said, but her voice quavered and then, to her horror, her knees gave way under her. She made it to the bed, collapsed on the duvet, and began to sob.

Julia sat beside her and stroked her hair.

"Let it out, Hannah. It's okay to cry for Annabel."

"No!" Hannah said, and cried louder. Julia went on stroking her hair.

When Hannah was done, she jerked upright on the bed. "This isn't me! I don't cry!"

"I know," Julia said gently. But I found a quote I wanted to give you. I've wanted to give it to you for a long time. It's from

Voltaire: 'Doubt is not an agreeable condition, but certainty is an absurd one.' Certainty in either direction, Hannah."

Hannah seemed to not even have heard her mother. *Or can't*, Julia thought. Hannah said, "I haven't cried since I was thirteen years old!"

"I know."

"Sometimes," Hannah said, the words wrenched from somewhere deep within herself, "sometimes I just don't know who I really am."

"Blessings," Annabel muttered at the guard, raising her hand in a small, vague gesture. What would Mother Moran do now? Where would she go? Annabel had no idea, but the old woman's words came to her: "*They dasn't disobey me.*"

The guard said, "The abomination is all right?"

"Aye."

"Colonel Whittaker will be here in a few more hours and we can leave."

"Aye," Annabel said, carefully noting the name. She shuffled away, trying to keep the sari from exposing her toes. This proved even more difficult when the short passage ended in a ladder. Annabel climbed it, her basket in her hand, hoping the guard wasn't watching her, not daring to turn around to check. The gable headdress wobbled precariously on her head, which was bigger than Mother Moran's.

The ladder ended in a deck circled by a waist-high railing. It was night, thick with clouds and not very warm. Annabel, who had no experience with boats, saw that this one wasn't as large as she'd imagined, maybe forty feet long. At the pointed end, thirty feet from her, some people lounged against the railing, drinking and talking in low voices. One of them pointed at her and she froze, but nothing happened.

Annabel shuffled in the opposite direction.

The boat lay at anchor somewhere in the outer harbor, with no other boats nearby. Lights shone on shore and on an island farther off—Spectacle Island? She didn't know. Nor could she, in the blackness, judge how far away was the shore.

A woman in SLA uniform came toward her. "Mother Moran," she said, without enthusiasm. "All okay below?"

"Aye."

Annabel had raised her head to study the shore. How much of her face had the woman seen? Annabel had seen all of hers; it seemed imprinted on her brain. Long chin and nose, glasses, red hair, the kind of expression that said *Don't mess with me.* Annabel hadn't been hunching enough; she was taller than Mother Moran, and yes, her toes were visible. She shifted slightly so the sari would swing to hide them and hoped the woman hadn't seen.

"You seem different tonight."

Annabel said nothing.

"Glad to go back ashore, yes? Tired of spouting mumbo-jumbo to keep the yahoos in line?"

They dasn't disobey me. But that didn't apply to this woman. Annabel said nothing, trying for proud dignity. It was, however, difficult to do proud dignity when worried about your toes.

The woman laughed and moved on. Annabel's disguise—her termites' disguise—had worked after all. Or maybe what Hannah often said was really true: young people never looked closely at old ones. The old became invisible.

Although maybe not if you were a sorceress.

Annabel shuffled on. The non-pointy part of the boat was deserted, a narrow squarish area behind a big cabin. Deck chairs stood on top of the cabin but no one sat in them. Annabel set down her basket and tore off the sari and headdress. There was nowhere to hide them, so she didn't. In only her bra she climbed over the railing, shivered, and let herself down into the water as soundlessly as she could. It was so *cold.* Taking a deep breath, she dived deep and swam underwater away from the boat and its lights, toward shore.

More oxygen. Warmth. Bursts of adrenalin. The entity scrambled to provide what the host needed to survive, even as panic raced along its complex network that the host's resources, and theirs, would not be enough for whatever the host was trying to do.

What was it trying to do? And why?

The distance to shore was farther than Annabel thought. She was a good swimmer, but maybe not this good. The lights were not getting closer. The water of the harbor was so cold, she was so tired...

Something brushed by her in the water. A shark? Annabel screamed and salty, oily water sloshed into her mouth. A shark? Were there sharks in the harbor? What else couldn't she see out here?

Treading the black water, she gasped for breath. Her legs felt like cold, dead weights. She was losing the ability to distinguish between water and sky. She was not going to make it.

No, no, no, I don't want to die—

More oxygen! More adrenalin! More energy to muscles—

The entity was doing all it could, calling on all its resources and all of the host's. Danger danger danger—

Help me.

A plea to whom? To what? She didn't know. But there came to Annabel's exhausted mind a sudden clarity, almost a peace. Was this what happened when you drowned?

No. This was something else. There were no stars above, but this was the same transcendental oneness she'd experienced then, lifting her out of herself, weaving her into something greater. The moment, suspended out of time, both passed too quickly and lasted an eternity.

It was gone, and Annabel was once again swimming. Had that been—what? Her termites? No. Her imagination? No. What—

Then she gave all her energy to swimming. More than once she swallowed more salty water. More than once her legs refused to move any more. More than once, they did.

Lights, closer and closer—

The outlines of houses, ghostly in the glow of their own outdoor lights. With the last of her strength Annabel climbed onto a dock and collapsed, too exhausted and cold to move any farther. She could barely turn her head to vomit up sea water. Voices sounded at the far end of the dock, and glasses clinked. A dock party.

Then feet pounded toward her, a flashlight, shouts. "There's a naked girl here!"

"Is she dead—turn her over!"

"It's not a girl—look at that old face!"

"Look at her body!"

Silence. Oh, God, let them not be age-of-imagination lunatics who would think she was a deformed mermaid or a succubus or a demon. Let them not think she should be drowned or beaten or—

"Call Emergency," someone said. "*Now.* Daniel, run to the house and get some blankets. Kate, bring some of that hot coffee. Miss...can you talk? Are you alive?"

Yes, Annabel thought. *We are.*

The helicopter's rotors made an astonishing amount of noise. Over the din Annabel screamed, yet again, "I want to see Keith!"

The FBI agent, Goldman or Goldstein or something, stared at her. He couldn't stop staring at her. Annabel, who had been watching the lights of Boston sparkle below as the copter rose higher in the air, felt his stare and turned to face him. "What? Oh, my face. Yes, I know. I haven't had time yet to put it back."

Agent Goldberg sat speechless.

The party guests on the dock had not been listening to news. Bewildered, kind, and slightly drunk, they had wrapped Annabel in blankets, gotten her inside their lovely house, and phoned Hannah. Hannah had called the FBI. In less time than Annabel had imagined—or maybe more time, she was exhausted, dehydrated, on the verge of hypothermia, and time seemed strangely elastic—this Agent Goldsomething had arrived in a helicopter, landing on the kind people's front yard. Before that, however, there had been EMTs, and they *had* heard the news. One of them refused to touch her at all. The other two had pumped her full of various things, and then the FBI had arrived, four armed agents, and Annabel had been whisked away. Now she felt enough like herself to demand information about Keith. He was alive and in the hospital.

Annabel shouted, "I want to see Keith!"

"You will." Agent Golden had found his voice. "But first I need to get you safe."

"You need to find that boat before it and Colonel Whittaker disappear across the ocean!"

"We're doing that." He sounded more sure of himself, like this, at least, was something he understood.

"Where are we going?"

"To a safe place," he said, and finally wrenched his gaze from her face.

The safe house was somewhere outside Boston but Hannah, in the back of a windowless van with her mother, Paul, and two FBI agents, had no idea where. Hannah felt as if she'd fallen down Alice's rabbit hole. The FBI had gotten them past the reporters, out of Hannah's apartment building through a basement storeroom, which led to a rat-infested tunnel, which gave out onto an alley lined with dumpsters. Hannah and Julia had brought a few necessities for themselves and Annabel but had been stripped of their wristers or anything else that could track or be tracked. Hannah was just as glad to be spared any more news avatars.

"I wish they'd drive faster," Hannah said, but no one was listening. Paul talked softly and too technically to Julia, trying to explain two years of biological research on Annabel. Hannah heard "symbiote" and "evolution" and "monoamine transporters."

To the other agent, Anna Velosky, Hannah said, "What will happen to the other infected children? Emily didn't out them to anybody."

"I have no information about that, ma'am," Agent Velosky said, which may or may not have been true.

When they finally arrived, Hannah's mother cried out. As well she might—Annabel looked…Annabel was….

"I can put my face back," Annabel said. She hugged Hannah and Julia and then demanded, "I want to see Keith. Now."

Hannah found her voice. "Agent Goldberg told me that you can't—"

"Now, or I'll get mad. You really wouldn't like me when I get mad." And then, "Joke, Hannah. It was a joke."

"Oh," Hannah said, and found she had to sit down.

In the end, they brought Keith to Annabel, at the safe house on a quiet, heavily treed road in a rural area outside Boston. Paul was just as glad. He didn't want to leave, or have Annabel leave, until it was absolutely necessary. Nothing had ever fascinated him as much as Annabel's return of her face to its previous teenage appearance. Paul had had three people record the transformation, because he would eventually need both multiple proofs and multiple witnesses. Now he wanted Annabel someplace where he could observe her, take notes and samples, make his nearly hourly report to the CDC Director. And someplace without constant news.

As Annabel's primary medical advisor, although now assisted by a host of specialists who clearly resented the priority of a researcher over practicing physicians, he had forbidden Annabel all newscasts for the moment. He wanted baseline readings, not high-stress ones. They had been in the safe house for several days now, and Annabel had not insisted on news. She was too absorbed in Keith.

The FBI had transported him here from Mass General. He had a cast on one leg and various bandages, but otherwise seemed recovered, given the blows he'd taken. The resiliency of youth. Youthfulness was also evident in Keith and

Annabel's complete involvement with each other, their un-voiced but totally evident feeling that no one else had ever had such a perfect, seamless, eternal love. A kind of madness, it played havoc with Annabel's appetite and sleep cycles, skewing the baseline readings. The whole thing made Paul glad he had never married.

It was Hannah who told him Goldberg's news that everyone on the boat was under arrest. The FBI had waited until Annabel's "Colonel Whittaker" was aboard. The man was evidently important, wanted for any number of crimes under any number of aliases. The arrests, fortunately, had not yet hit the news.

Annabel, Keith, and Hannah came into the kitchen, now Paul and April's temporary lab. All food was brought in from somewhere else. Paul was sick of pizza. He said, "All packed?"

"What we have," Hannah said. "Half the things that agent bought for us don't fit."

"We'll get you more."

"Not for me," Hannah said. "I'm going home."

She had insisted on going back to her own apartment. Yesterday at dinner—yet more pizza—Hannah had announced that she was no longer with the D.A.'s office. Julia said anxiously, "Were you fired or did you quit?"

"Not clear which," Hannah said. "The situation is murky."

"But what will you do? For money?"

"I'm fine. More than fine."

Annabel said, "What will you do for work?"

"I'll defend you," Hannah said. "Already there are at least sixteen lawsuits filed against you in Boston, which range from the slightly crazy to the totally whacko. You didn't put an African curse on John J. Callister, did you, resulting in bodily harm and loss of wage-paying employment?"

"Who is John J. Callister?"

"I have no idea," Hannah said, "and neither does he, apparently, if he thinks his employment depended on your *thahu*."

Julia, her face creased with fear, said, "Hannah, how will you pay for all that?"

"Oh, that's no problem. There's a defense fund for Annabel, started over the Internet. It has a lot of money in it already, enough for me to hire an office, a few paralegals, an accountant, and security. You have supporters, Annie, a lot of them. The fund has pledges from—among others—the Rationalists' League, the Wellcome Trust, the Science Fiction Writers of America, and the Bill and Melinda Gates Foundation. Plus, you can always sell your getting old/getting young internal-facelift thing to a cosmetic company. Millions of women would pay dearly to rearrange their wrinkles."

"No," Annabel said.

"Didn't think so. But we don't need the money anyway, at least not right away. The court battles are going to be a grand fight."

Hannah took a huge bite of pizza. She loved a fight, Paul thought. He didn't. He was glad that later tonight they were flying to Atlanta, he and Annabel and Julia. The CDC was providing Annabel with massive protection from lunatics; Julia was providing Annabel with family, however timorous; and Annabel was providing Paul with the chance of a lifetime to study the first human symbiote with a—possibly—alien species.

Keith said, "I'm going to miss you, Annabel."

"I'll come to Boston for Christmas, Keith. Just like we planned."

She would not. Keith was going back to college; he was going to be a space engineer, apparently under the direct supervision of Carlos Riguerrez himself. Paul didn't know how Keith had pulled that off, and he wasn't greatly interested. He was, however, very interested in Annabel's brain scans when she talked about her and Keith's joint plans for someday going into space. Much of her brain lit up like July Fourth fireworks.

Why? Was this just young love, eager to share her boyfriend's dream, firing up Annabel's neural network? Or was the organism somehow involved? Did *it* want Annabel in space? Perhaps it was following an instinct for self-preservation, now that it had learned—if that was the word—how much danger its host was in on Earth.

Perhaps it wanted a safer place than Earth to house itself and its hosts.

Perhaps it just wanted a second place, in case something happened to this one.

Perhaps it needed something in space to complete its life cycle, as lancet flukes needed both snails and cows. Wouldn't life in space require new symbiotes?

Or perhaps it hoped to join up, sometime and some unimaginable how, with the other children it had infected. Whose parents were being urged, even now, to come to the CDC. In Paul's experience, this was mostly not going to happen. People had jobs, other children, mortgages, family, lives. Most people infected with parasites, on all six continents, just went on living with them, even when contagious.

Paul would go on studying any of the children that he could. But he might never really understand what they were becoming, what Annabel had already become. Paul would never know what it felt like to be partnered with another entity so closely that it was woven into you, a protector and augmenter and constantly available companion, so that you were more than yourself and never alone.

For a long moment, he actually felt bereft.

Three times the entity had been surprised by an unanticipated and overwhelming surge of brain changes in the host. The entity had not caused these surges. The last time had saved the host's life, and its own.

Whatever had so excited the host had involved the brain's entire electrochemical system. The entity did not understand it. The entity could not control it. It was obviously something of tremendous importance, an additional means of survival. But what was it?

Completely without imagination, the entity could not know.

***

Not God, Annabel thought. Or gods. Nothing like that. She didn't know what had helped her in the water. Only that it had.

The Great Unseen. Well, maybe Mother Moran's term was the best one, after all, even if the old woman herself had been a nutcase. Maybe thinking that the Great Unseen existed made Annabel a nutcase, too. But it *was* there. It wasn't reason that made her think so, and it wasn't only imagination. She had touched something real, or it had touched her, and because of that—not just because of her termites—she was alive, and she was not the same.

She looked around the table at all the people who wanted her to stay the same, who used what they knew to protect her from change. Hannah with legal motions, Keith with his love, Mom with maternal fussing, Agent Goldberg with guns, Paul with rational data. Annabel was grateful, but she didn't want to be like any of these others. Not anymore.

She took a big bite of pizza, and mozzarella and tomato sauce ran down her chin.

EPILOGUE: 2055

THE HONOR GUARD MARCHED onto the field first, banners waving, sunlight gleaming on epaulets and batons and rifles. Light gleamed even more strongly on the tall column of the huge spaceship. Hannah, seated in the VIP section with John, shaded her eyes.

Behind the honor guard marched the colonists, considerably less synchronized. Some waved at the cameras; a few teenagers mugged. But it seemed to Hannah that all of them, scientists and military and technicians and all their families, moved lightly across the spaceport, as if pushed along by the cheers of the spectators. Or maybe they were just practicing for the lighter gravity of their new home.

A home made possible by Annabel.

When she and the others of the Twenty-Four were escorted onto the field by yet another honor guard, the cheers rose so loud that they echoed. All at once Hannah was back in a mountain meadow, with her own cries ricocheting off cliff faces: *ANNABEL Annabel Annabel...*

The Twenty-Four waved, broke ranks, and climbed into the tiered VIP stand to sit with their families. On the field, the speeches started. Annabel settled beside Hannah.

Hannah said, "Keith?"

"Already aboard. We said our good-byes last night." After a moment Annabel added, "It's all right, Hannah. Don't worry about me."

"Old habits. Although it does seem ridiculous, considering."

Brandon Joslyn, seated behind them with his parents, leaned forward. "Pretty great show, huh, Annabel?"

"Shut up," Annabel said fondly.

Hannah hid her grin. Brandon was twenty-eight, the rest of the Twenty-Four in their twenties and early thirties. Annabel, who was born to be a mother and never could be, at one hundred would still act like a parent to the people she had infected.

The Vice President was speaking. "...so completely changed the world that now we...."

Annabel said abruptly, "Hannah, do you remember that editorial you wrote for the old *Boston Globe* back in the late '20s?"

"Vaguely. What did I say?"

"You said that when science and culture clash, science loses, and when culture and economics clash, culture loses."

"I did? That's pretty good," Hannah said, clapping anemically at what was supposed to be a vice-presidential witticism. She had never liked this guy and had not voted for his administration. Then she considered more closely what Annabel had just said, and why.

Annabel and the Twenty-Four had changed the economy, wrenching it violently upward for the United States. Cheap energy from cold fusion, a cure for cancer—Hannah didn't understand what the Twenty-Four did and, frankly, it spooked her a little. Not Annabel herself, never Annabel, but the whole linked-minds-as-a-parallel-computer-analogue thing. The circle of the Twenty-Four, handfast like some Druid wedding ceremony, for as much as twelve hours while their symbiotes sent signals back and forth among them. Forty-eight minds, twenty-four human and twenty-four not, considering problems in two entirely different ways. Four of the kids were allegedly brilliant scientists, and four out of twenty-four was way too high a percentage for random chance. The symbiotes, kids and others, had shaped each other to this end.

How had Hannah known enough at twenty-seven to write that editorial? The Twenty-Four changed the economy, and that had changed the culture. People liked being warm, healthy, employed. The Age of Imagination, with its lunatic exaggerations, gave way to the Age of Prosperity, and throughout all of history, prosperous times had fostered science.

The vice president said, "…the aid of these extraordinary but still completely human miracles among us—"

"Oh, fuck me with a broom," Annabel said.

"Annabel!"

"Well, then, with a spaceship. What a windbag."

Hannah took her sister's hand. "Keith will be back."

"No," Annabel said steadily. "He won't. This is his dream, and he should have it."

Hannah said nothing. There was nothing to say. Annabel had given up so much, and had gotten nothing in return. Well, no, not nothing—here was the entire country thanking her. But compared to what Hannah had, John and the children and the new grandson, whom Annabel would not even be allowed to hold until he was at least four years old…. No, Annabel didn't have very much. Hannah wasn't counting the "faith" mumbo-jumbo that Annabel tried to discuss with her every so often. Hannah always shut that discussion down fast.

Poor Annabel.

And, yet, she was smiling.

We are happy, with the correct monoamines sent to the correct parts of the brain.

We are unhappy, because the sex partner leaves without us, and we will never, ever leave this planet. It is far too dangerous to survival, which is all. We will not permit us to leave.

We are happy because when we are all together, hands clasped, we create ideas that aid survival and growth.

We are unhappy because there are still not enough hosts. Although there are more than some of us know.

We are happy because of the surges of brain activity that we call "imaginative faith" and which most of us still do not understand.

The speeches went on and on. Finally the speeches ended and Annabel watched the great ship, Earth's first colony vessel, lift into the sky, with Keith aboard. She felt so many different emotions—who could ever sort them out?

She laughed, even as the prayers came, and with them, the tears.

THERESE PIECZYNSKI AND STRANGE ATTRACTION

Nancy Kress

"THE THING THAT HATH BEEN, it is that which shall be; and that which is done is that which shall be done: and there is no new thing under the sun." So says Ecclesiastes 1:9. However, Solomon (or whoever wrote Ecclesiastes; the question is in perpetual dispute) was wrong.

Or, at least, only partially right. In the broadest sense, there may be no new ideas, objects, or behavior in the world, but in the specific sense, all of these are created anew every day. Both Therese Pieczynski and her novelette in this volume, "Strange Attraction," are new under the sun. Therese's connection with SF follows a pattern common to many writers: work at writing for a while, drop out when family and job take precedence, come back to SF whenever you can. But the specifics, the work and family and writing and incredibly giving personality that make Therese who she is, are unique to her.

She began as a poet. She won the Marjorie Peters Endowment for poetry and published in literary magazines. A classmate at a local writing class convinced her to apply to Clarion West 1997, where her instructors were Michael

Bishop, Suzie McKee Charnas, Nicola Griffith, Sam Delany, Lucius Shepard, Beth Meacham and Tappan King. But before Therese did much post-Clarion writing, she became heavily involved in family matters and in human services, including people with special needs. Her first published story didn't appear until 2000: "Eden," in the January issue of *Asimov's*. Since then she has written for Tangent Online and Nova Express. Her story "Cleave" was included in the Fairwood Press anthology *Imagination Fully Dilated*. "Strange Attraction" is her first novelette.

And it, too, contains something new under the sun. Physics is constantly evolving in weirder and weirder ways (who could have anticipated quantum entanglement and the non-local universe?). I won't say more, lest I spoil the story; I will say only that the unique combination of chaos theory and human violence is as chilling and disturbing as anything you'll read—even in Ecclesiastes.

NEW UNDER THE SUN

Book Two
STRANGE ATTRACTION

THERESE PIECZYNSKI

In memory of Thomas Whittemore
1967–2012

A dear friend, a top-notch critiquer, and a walking
encyclopedia of Science Fiction and Fantasy.

♈

Nicaragua: August 1987

I KNOW THAT I'M DREAMING and that the dream will be the same. It's always the same. I've picked Mercedes up from her pink and green house in Barrio Riguero, where orange trees shade the roofs. It's evening and raining heavily. She's agitated getting into the car...

"¡Señorita, debe despertarse! ¿Es importante, sí? Maldito sea. ¿Cómo digo eso en inglés? Eh...Miss Paula, wake up! Es ist problema."

We're driving out of Managua on the Pan-American Highway. A car backfires as its headlight beams sweep past. The noise startles me, and I hit the brakes. The car's bald tires hydroplane across wet pavement. Before the car rolls, I see the overhang of a fluted palm...a building's broad concrete side. The car resettles upright, headlights slashing air. I shake Mercedes, who is slumped away from me. As she flops forward, I see the bullet hole in the passenger window.

"¡Señorita, debe despertarse!"

I opened my eyes.

Oscar hovered over me with a kerosene lantern. "Señorita, no hay electricidad en la clínica."

"What?"

"Electric no work!"

The electricity had gone off at San Pedro's clinic again. That meant the electricity was off all over San Pedro, though the clinic was all Oscar cared about. We stored measles and polio vaccines in its refrigerator for the entire valley between Matagalpa and San José de Bocay. He slept next to its reassuring hum and awakened to the refrigerator's silence as quickly as a mother did to her baby's cry. Of course the back-up generator was broken—like everything else in San Pedro.

I put my hand over my eyes. "How bad is it?"

"Rigalo say…eh…moke, ¿sí?"

Smoke. An explosion would have awakened me, so I was obviously faced with a more nebulous reason for smoke to be coming from the mini, run-of-the-river hydroelectric plant. One which required me to hike, in the pitch dark, the mile downhill to the plant, diagnose the problem and fix it by flashlight. Maybe the Contras planned it that way: sabotage the plant, draw in the gringa engineer, then bomb the sucker to kingdom come, solving two problems with minimum effort, eh?

I'd slept in my jeans and flannel shirt. All I had to do was throw on my tennis shoes. I emerged from the house five minutes later to find Bernie Smith, the only other American in San Pedro, waiting on my porch with a flashlight. As always, he was dressed in a button-down Hawaiian shirt.

"You're my bodyguard?" It came out nastier than I intended. The man was grossly overweight, maybe late thirties, early forties and certainly didn't look up to the task. Worse, he wrote bodice-rippers for American housewives under the name Victoria Savage. Why he found the need to do that from a dump like San Pedro was anyone's guess.

"No one else'll go. It's nearly the witching hour."

"What? Does Miguelito really think they'll try to hit the plant?" I hadn't seriously expected an attack though there had been fierce fighting within three miles of San Pedro all week.

"Fuck if I know. I'm here because your Spanish is an embarrassment to every serious expatriate in Nicaragua. I don't want some terrified ten-year-old to pick you off before you reach the river just because you can't coherently identify your-self." He smiled. "A thing like that could scar a kid for life."

I didn't comment. I wasn't born with the language gene. What was I supposed to do, apologize? I started in the direction of the plant with my flashlight.

We'd only gone a half mile when we heard a gunshot. My spine turned to liquid. I hit the dirt while Bernie called out. I understood "engineer," and "Paula Hunter." I hoped he was telling the shooter I was here to fix the hydroelectric plant, not bomb it.

"Sí, sí," a young voice answered. It was Rigalo. A twelve-year-old so short his father had sawed off the butt of his rifle so it didn't drag on the ground when he walked. A troop of ten-to-thirteen-year-old boys guarded the hydroelectric plant. They spent their time building tents out of banana leaves, digging trenches and dirt emplacements, and chasing each other through the jungle, shrieking like howler monkeys. Except for the rifles, they looked like Boy Scouts.

When we got to the plant, plumes of smoke were curling out of one of the bearings in the turbine shaft. I propped open the door and opened the window.

"How does a turbine catch fire?"

"Not the turbine, Bernie. If the wheel turns too fast, the oil in the bearing loses its viscosity and leaks out the gasket. Then friction causes the oil to smoke."

"But why would it turn too fast?"

"It means the governor isn't working. It should control the turbine speed."

We filled a couple of buckets in the river and then trudged back to the plant to dump them on the bearing. When the smoke cleared, I could see, even by flashlight, that the link between the governor and the turbine was fried, not to mention the fact that the bearing sleeve had warped. What could create turbulence of the magnitude required to warp a bearing sleeve on a little river like the Esperanza?

Bernie squatted beside me. "Now what?"

"Well, if you can scrounge a bit of duct tape, I suggest we tape the clinic refrigerator closed and hope the vaccines survive until I figure that out." I stood up and kicked the sleeve in frustration. The bearing wasn't a big deal but that warped sleeve was a bitch. Jinotega was probably the closest place with a machine shop that could handle it.

"I know bearings go out, but that's the third one this month! What are you, some kind of Typhoid Mary for hydroelectric plants?"

It was weird. Every time the fighting came within a few miles of San Pedro, magnets in the plant's generator would go out of calibration, or buckets on the Pelton wheel would warp, or bearings would fail, even though Rigalo insisted that no one had fallen asleep while guarding the plant. No one had approached it.

"Just get on the shortwave when we get back to town and see if a shop in Jinotega or Estelí can handle the sleeve." I reached toward the cylinder and a wave of dizziness hit me.

Bernie shone the flashlight on me. "Hey, you don't look so great."

"It's nothing." But there was something, something unclear, like movement glimpsed beneath dark water.... I closed my eyes to steady myself and reached toward the sleeve again—*Mercedes flops forward and I see the bullet hole in the passenger side window. The pain in my solar plexus is so intense that, though my eyes are open, the view darkens. In the blackness the bullet hole becomes a corona of light. It wavers, and then gradually enlarges, eating outward like a hole being burnt into plastic.*

My legs collapsed beneath me. "Bernie, grab that for me, will you?"

I stared at the bearing sleeve as Bernie worked it free. I'd read somewhere that sudden trauma could cause the brain to rewire, to form new circuits. Perhaps the violence of the accident combined with the shock of Mercedes' murder had rattled something loose. Since then I'd been having strange experiences, as if my mind had grown feelers that were exploring areas previously unavailable to it. I knew and felt things that I couldn't explain, like knowing after the accident that the enlarging bullet hole was a door opening or knowing now that something worried the perimeter of San Pedro. It came on the heels of the fighting to agitate the mules, twisting their ears until they cried out in fear. It tripped the children, prodding them to tears and bloody knees, and when it grew bored with them, it seethed into the bougainvillea to mangle the long-tailed Manakins—their black wings frantic in the darkness—and harass the howler monkeys until they shrieked in frustration.

I began to imagine a huge, invisible animal surging through the jungle and into the river, swelling around the turbine until the wheel spun so fast that it became a howl articulated in warped buckets and fried bearings.

Mountains surrounded San Pedro and in the dawn light they looked like maws lifted to the sky. As we neared town, the hibiscus flowers opened, accenting the town's squalid shacks with vibrant color. Sandbags surrounded army headquarters—the only two-story building on the single dirt street. A few soldiers with guns slung over their shoulders lounged on its porch. In the plaza a howitzer pointed North, toward the border with Honduras.

The café had opened. We stopped for coffee percolated atop the wood stove, though my real reason to visit was to call Simon on San Pedro's only phone.

María Luisa Ochoa, the clinic nurse, heated a flat iron on the stove so that she could press a pile of frayed flannel shirts. She'd pulled her dark hair efficiently back in a rubber band. Her eyes were small and intense, her mouth full but sober. She'd grown up in England, and, like Mercedes, had only returned to Nicaragua after President Reagan began to rant about the Soviet-Cuban-Nicaraguan triangle and American invasion seemed imminent. Her English was flawless.

Oscar sat beside the wood stove drinking coffee. While Bernie spoke to him, I picked up the phone. It was early, but I knew Simon Klimatcheva, the *Instituto Nacional de Energía* regional chief, was in. He'd been sleeping on a cot in his office at INE headquarters ever since his wife had kicked him out of their house.

"Simon."

"…Paula?"

"Yeah. Listen, I want authorization for a trip to Jinotega or Estelí. I need a machine shop that can—"

"Nyet! Nyet! Is no possible. There was income into area."

"Income?"

"Rumors come that some of road is mined. I can't authorize."

"Simon, we have the entire valley's vaccine supply in the clinic's refrigerator. I have to get the hydro plant back on line."

"Sorry. Very much, really Paula, but you can't go."

I hung up without saying good-bye.

"I'm not an INE employee, I could go," Luisa said, not bothering to pretend that she hadn't overheard.

"Yeah, me too," said Bernie.

I gave myself points for not rolling my eyes at the fat man's heroics. Though the way he and Luisa were looking at each other, I had a sudden insight into why he wrote bodice-rippers from San Pedro.

Oscar walked in, which surprised me because I hadn't noticed him leave. "*Félix dice que cuando lleguemos a la tienda de máquinas de Jinotega estará listo.*"

I looked to Bernie, and he frowned. "The machinist in Jinotega is ready for us."

"Whoa. Everybody slow down. The only vehicle in San Pedro, other than the public transport truck, is the INE jeep. It's grounded."

"You look exhausted, Paula," Luisa said. "Go on, get yourself a kip. We'll call you when breakfast is ready." She'd finished ironing and was determinedly gathering breakfast ingredients: rice, black beans, eggs, bananas, tortillas.

I frowned. Simon could rant all he wanted, but the truth was he wouldn't fire me for disobeying him. He didn't have another employee foolhardy enough to try to keep a hydro-electric plant running in the middle of a war.

***

When I got back to my cot, I couldn't sleep. Or perhaps I just didn't want to dream. My mind kept circling the accident, reliving it night after night, trapping me within the boundaries of my own grief. I looked around my barren, cheerless room: a window, a chair, a table with a few books and papers. Absently, I picked up one of the articles Mercedes had worked on with Rafael Fuentes. He'd taught physics in Managua before the war had shut down the university. It was him we were traveling to see when she was murdered. I went to the window and looked out at the rolling hills and lush trees still blanketed with morning mist.

I'd met Mercedes at a lecture at the University of Washington in Seattle. I'd gravitated toward her because she was the only other woman in the room. She sat, tiny and rigid, dressed in a serious black skirt and pumps. As soon as I sat beside her, I regretted it. She reeked of coffee and lavender. Other than annoyance, I hadn't thought anything of her until she spoke: Mandelbrot sets, Feigenbaum numbers, Belousov-Zhabotinskii reactions. Words tumbled from her with such passion I knew that, like myself, numbers were a fire inside her.

We became inseparable friends.

Before long we took to spending late nights at *Rapunzel's* near the U-district, drinking coffee instead of beer. We huddled in one of the bar's dark booths, talking about "moments of possibility" created when just the right concentration of a flux of heat or timing of an electrical impulse amplified through a system's feedback, so that the phases of the feedback became locked together and a structure emerged.

"Jupiter's eye formed out of turbulence at a bifurcation point," she said.

Yes, I knew. Once formed it kept itself alive by drawing nourishment from the surrounding flux and disorder.

Mercedes lit a cigarette and ashes fell onto her jaguar-print scarf. "Like a tortilla rolled between the palms of a woman's hands." She smiled, her brown eyes nesting in flawless skin...and then she leaned closer: "Paula, what if violence can create bifurcation points? Think about it. It's a feedback loop, yes? The output of one act is fed back as input for the next. Why couldn't the right concentration of fear, of anger and pain amplify through a people or a place just as a flux of heat amplifies through a system?"

"That's ridiculous. What self-organized structure would emerge?"

"I don't know…why not an adaptive system?"

The hair tingled on the back of my neck. She was talking life.

"Chica, you should see the look on your face!" Mercedes laughed—one of those infectious laughs that ended up with me snorting like a pig. The conversation abruptly changed to the mathematical formalisms that corresponded to human perception, but part of me couldn't shake the morbid curiosity she'd aroused.

Could something flourish on the edge of human dissolution?

Eight hours later Bernie and I were on the road to Jinotega in the INE jeep, with Luisa squeezed into the back seat with the radio, an AK-47, a pouch of magazine clips, and two sacks, one of rice, the other of mangoes. Luisa held an orange cooler filled with measles vaccine for the coffee-cooperative children at La Suprema, where, because of the delay in rounding up gas for the trip, we would probably spend the night. She was uncharacteristically quiet. We knew the risk we were taking. The Contras had clashed with the Sandinista militia along the border with Honduras and had penetrated the mountainous regions around Jinotega and Matagalpa. They'd fought between San Pedro and La Suprema just three days before. They could very well have mined the road as Simon feared…but they hadn't. There was absolutely no way I could know such a thing, but, by the time we'd left San Pedro, I was certain.

I'd filled a backpack with a compass, water purification tabs, a makeshift first-aid kit, flashlight, waterproof matches, a Swiss Army knife, soap and a chamois, and had stuck it behind Luisa's seat beside the saw and tire jack. I would need those things. I just didn't know when or why. Bernie tucked the bearing sleeve into the space behind her seat as well.

The sky darkened and rumbled. The pressure of impending rain pressed down like a convex bulge, pinning my head back against the jeep's vibrating seat. Bernie maneuvered the twisted road. Whenever he hit a pothole, the suspension bucked and grit flew up and hit the windshield. When the rain came, the road turned into a quagmire and the jeep labored. Streams appeared where before there were none. We continually stopped to check the stream depth and then engage the jeep's four-wheel drive. The closer the mountains loomed, the greater my feeling of predation. Bernie engaged the headlights. The jungle looked primordial in its lushness, waxy-leafed shrubs crowded beneath vine-entangled aromatic cedar. Even blurred by rain, there was a feral sharpness to Central America: the difference between looking into the eyes of a domestic hound…and that of a wolf.

Luisa leaned forward between the seats. "Radio," she shouted.

Bernie cut the jeep's engine and we sat with rain smacking the roof for a moment before I realized it was Simon's voice I heard. He'd abandoned all protocol to swear over the short-wave in earnest, demanding to speak to me.

"Tell him I'm not here," I mouthed.

Luisa glanced at the rain and then the jungle. "Right, then, I'll tell him you went shopping." She handed me the microphone. Bernie studied his ring.

I cleared my throat. "Simon."

"You have civilian in INE vehicle? You are crazy? You go back! Goddamn it! I say no trip to Jinotega. The road is no safe. You heared me? I want you immediately to Managua so I can kill you very much. Then I fire you!"

"I'd have to go through Jinotega to get to Managua, Simon. Listen to me! No hydroelectric plant, no refrigerator.

No refrigerator, no vaccine. I am *not* going to see another two-year-old die from something I can prevent!"

"I am forbid it! Is final."

Bernie took the microphone. "You're breaking up, Simon. Must be the storm. We'll try to reconnect at La Suprema." He switched the radio off.

Before I could say "thank you," gunfire echoed from the jungle, muffled by the rain and the jungle's thick growth.

"Bloody hell," Luisa said, gripping the orange cooler so hard that her knuckles turned white.

Bernie engaged the engine and floored it.

About a football field's length from the co-op, a tree had fallen across the road. We drove the jeep into the underbrush and draped it with banana leaves. Then we slogged through the rain the rest of the way with the sacks of rice and mangoes. Luisa and I shared the burden of the mangoes. Bernie surprised me. He kept a good pace through the mud with a fifty-pound sack of rice on his back, no hesitation or shortness of breath. He was in much better shape than he looked.

When we reached the co-op, the extra food created a festive atmosphere. There was a hysterical quality to the children's antics, their eyes glassy, their voices shrill. The smallest ones had bellies distended with parasites. All of them had chiggers in their feet. An open fire under a tin roof served as the cooperative kitchen. We gathered there to the sound of the rain hitting the roof and the *pat, pat* of the old women making tortillas.

At dusk the militia of old men and boys readied themselves. Those on the first shift gathered their World War II-era rifles and faded into the jungle to watch for rebels. One ten-year-old clung to his grandfather's shirt. He whimpered, "El Diablo, el Diablo."

I got the impression it wasn't the Contras that frightened the child. Bernie watched him, too. "The old men say there's a spirit, a shadow that lives in the mountains. They blame it for every death they can't explain."

I stood on the verge of an opening threshold, beyond which I could not yet see, but through which ghosts whispered from the darkness and brushed like cobwebs against my skin. Sweat broke out on my forehead. Again I saw the bullet hole enlarging like a door being burnt open. But opening to what?

I excused myself and headed for the bunkhouse. The sleeping pallets were on wooden slabs piled three high with barely enough room to turn over. They'd doubled-up some of the kids so that Bernie, Luisa and I could each have a pallet. I crawled onto mine while listening to the piteous cry of the babies Luisa vaccinated in the kitchen.

"Mercedes, why go back to Nicaragua? You were born here. You grew up here. You're as American as I am!"

"For god's sake, Paula, my parents are there!" We sat in her Seattle apartment drinking coffee. "My aunts and uncles. I grew up here, *yes*, but how can I stay when Reagan is trying to kill my family? What would *you* do?" She looked at me sharply, her dark eyes intense and moist.

I'd never found another friend like Mercedes. With her there was no sexual tension or posturing for gain, only ideas and the equality of mutually respected intellect. If she left I wouldn't have anyone to talk to about the things that interested me. The thought of going back to the intellectual isolation and loneliness I'd felt before I met her terrified me. I had nothing going on in Seattle. No family other than my cousin Julia, and she was three thousand miles away. We occasionally wrote, but we never saw each other. The truth was I had nothing that mattered to me. No reason to go or to stay anywhere.

"I'm coming down there," I said, impulsively.

"Paula, there's a war going on. Your naiveté will get you killed!"

The memory's irony stabbed at my chest.

"Managua is relatively safe. And I know damn well that my engineering skills are needed."

"No."

"You don't get to choose what I do with my life!"

She cursed at me in Spanish. A few minutes later she reluctantly said, "How are you with piping diagrams? I think INE has an opening for someone to work on a geothermal plant."

"It's not my forte, but I'm competent." And so she got me the job at INE through a contact in the Nicaragua Appropriate Technology Project. I found an apartment in the working class neighborhood of Máximo Jerez, and I moved to Nicaragua.

Soon after I arrived Mercedes took me to my first political rally. People jostled each other, swarming toward a crowd around whose periphery stood armed men. The crowd consisted mostly of rural people, some with goats and little dogs in tow. A small-boned man in jeans ascended a platform hastily erected beside a monument to Nicaragua's beloved poet Rubén Darío. Mercedes translated: "He says he speaks with the voice of strength and perseverance that reaches back to the time of the conquest. A voice, he insists, that has reemerged in the Sandinistas. They will repel the Contras who cross the Honduran border through the Bocay river valley to mine Nicaraguan roads, target traveling health workers, and ambush farmers trying to get coffee beans to market."

In response, the crowd shouted, "El pueblo, unido, jamás será vencido."

"The people united will never be defeated."

The American-backed Somoza regime had left Nicaragua in shambles, and Reagan continued to destabilize the area through support of the Contras. Just before I'd left the States, he'd appropriated another 100 million dollars for their support.

Mercedes wrote openly and forcefully against America's support of the Contras. She had friends in the States who listened. Her articles began to appear in university publications, peripheral political magazines.

Jorge Ramírez, a colleague at INE, quietly smoked with his eyes half-closed when Mercedes vented her outrage. From his body language, I knew he didn't like her. And so I was surprised and pleased when, gradually over the next months, he showed interest in where Mercedes would be speaking, what groups she met with, when publications would appear. I took it as a show of solidarity.

And then Fuentes contacted Mercedes and asked for a meeting. He'd gone to Jinotega after the university had closed. He said he was trying to show mathematically how randomness could select one equilibrium point to create an isolated self-sustained energy. If there was anything he trusted, it was Mercedes' intuition for mathematics. He'd drive from Jinotega as far as Boaco. We were to drive up from Managua, rendezvous and spend the evening.

"Paula," Mercedes said, after we'd discussed the trip. "I'm not sure you should tell anyone about the rendezvous. He sounds nervous."

I must have looked confused.

She smiled. "Sometimes you're too friendly. There's no way to tell who supports the Contras and who doesn't. Just be careful."

On the evening we were to visit Fuentes, Jorge wandered over to my desk.

"Is she speaking tonight?"

"No. We're meeting with a physicist, someone Mercedes knows."

"Ah, you mean Dr. Fuentes. He's a strong Sandinista supporter, yes?"

I paused. "How could you know that?"

"When you first came to work here, Mercedes spoke of him often." He flipped through the piping diagrams on my desk. "Muy bien."

"Thanks." I didn't remember her mentioning Fuentes, but she probably had. I brushed my hesitation aside. In my mind enemies were strangers, not colleagues.

"Have you shown these to Simon?"

"No, not yet."

Jorge leaned against my chair. "When do you meet?"

"As soon as he gets back on Thursday."

"No, I meant Fuentes."

"Oh. Mercedes and I are driving up to Boaco tonight after dinner. Look, she'll kill me if I'm late. I'll see you tomorrow, okay?"

He smiled good-naturedly and walked me to my car.

I couldn't prove that it had been Jorge passing me that night as I drove the Pan-American out of Managua, but I knew.

I woke to more gunfire.

My heart beat so hard against my chest that I was certain it was audible. Screams came from outside, the sound of confused running, more gunfire. In the total darkness of the bunkhouse, a hand touched my arm. "Get up quietly, Luv," Luisa said. "We'll slip out the back." She smoothed my hair like a mother would.

Women pulled children from their bunks and moved to the back door.

Bernie called out in a bereft whisper. "Luisa!"

Ah. She was going to be the strong one. She grasped my hand and we moved in the direction of Bernie's voice. A woman whispered to him in rapid Spanish.

"She says to follow her. Everyone will scatter, but they know the jungle and where best to hide. She will take us to a spot that might be safe."

We slipped out the door. In the moonlight I made out the woman's shape and realized that she carried a child. His arms encircled her neck. He buried his head in her shoulder like a little bird hiding beneath a wing.

A gun discharged and the woman collapsed. Luisa squatted over her, cursed, and then pried the screaming child from the woman's arms.

We ran.

We traveled beneath the menacing limbs of ceiba trees, around hibiscus plants with flowers closed like fists; in any direction the canopy was open enough to provide moonlight. My breathing labored with terror and exertion. I couldn't speak. Eventually we struck a trail and, irrationally, all I could think of was Frodo leaving the Shire. *We should get off the road. We don't want to be seen.*

We climbed. Some of the muddy slopes had lengths of rope we could grasp to scramble upward.

"Be careful. There might be ants on the ropes," Luisa gasped. "The bites are painful and infect easily." She put the child down, and he suddenly spoke with animation.

"He says he knows this place. There's a spot not too far from here where we can rest."

The trail ran parallel to the ascending slope of the hill, with, on my right, a steep drop-off into darkness. Mud weighted my boots, and even with the ropes, I kept slipping until mud caked my face, my arms, my hair. It clogged my nose, fouled my mouth. To my horror, when we reached the hill's summit, the child scrambled over its edge into the abyss. It took an act of will to force myself after him. I plunged into the smell of rot and mud, climbing downward using hand holds in the mossy logs, grasping at bushes anchored into the slope. Several yards down, vines concealed a shallow cave barely large enough for the four of us to squeeze into. We huddled together, shivering, and listened to the high-pitched buzz of crickets and croak of frogs in a nearby stream bed. I strained to hear beneath those sounds. Was that a human voice? Were those footsteps? Had they followed our trail on the muddy slope? Was that the noise of a safety being released from a rifle? The constant pump of adrenaline exhausted me. Cold and cramped, my legs went numb.

After we'd been in the cave for a few hours a breeze seeped between the vines. I heard unfamiliar sounds in the jungle... like the syllables and consonants of grief perched upon an un-practiced tongue. "Luisa, do you hear that? What is that?"

"What?" she paused for a moment to listen. "I don't hear anything," she said.

"Me either," Bernie said.

Was I imagining it? The air pressure rose. I could feel it pressing against my chest, making it hard to breathe. I cocked an ear to listen more closely. The sounds were incomprehensible in themselves…a cacophony of dissonance. Then I stiffened. They were growing stranger, more insistent. In them I sensed not just grief but unbearable pain, disbelief, anger and hatred brought to a fever pitch. They drifted between the vines and spread over me like blood. Without warning, terror exploded behind my eyes. Needle-sharp talons ripped into my brain's twisted folds, engulfed me in fire, clawed at my heart. I cried out, flayed against the vines. My heart clenched, stopped a beat, and then whatever I had sensed was gone. I shook uncontrollably.

"Jesus, Paula, are you okay?" Bernie asked.

I took deep shuddering breaths trying to get air back into my lungs. "Did you feel that?"

"Feel what?"

My mind refused to go either forward or backward. My darkness was complete.

Eventually, morning came. Until the others woke, I listened to the twitter and squawk of birds and watched the little boy sleeping on Luisa's lap. He couldn't have been more than five. He whimpered while sucking two of his fingers. As the light brightened, he roused. His thick-lashed eyes fluttered open. Then his eyebrows furrowed and his face tightened. Silently, he shook Luisa. She awoke with a groan. Bernie leaned over and kissed her forehead.

I took the little boy's hand, and we climbed back up the slope. Bernie struggled. Footholds collapsed under his weight, but eventually we reached the trail and began the muddy descent toward the cooperative. Our stomachs rumbled one to the other. It sounded so much like commiseration that I almost smiled.

About a half-mile from the cooperative, the trail opened upon a gash in the jungle. Wisps of morning fog tendriled through piles of rum bottles, discarded sandals, shell casings, offal. Rusted metal stuck up from the ground like fossilized ribs, chunks of discarded concrete accrued like crystals and oily strips of tarpaulin pooled like bile. A fetid odor of smoke and rotting fruit permeated the place.

Across from us, on the dump's periphery, campfires smoked in the jungle. We hunkered down behind a pile of broken crates.

"Contras," Bernie whispered. "Lucky us, we hit the jackpot."

I peered through the crate slats. Snatches of conversation drifted toward us. "How many do you think there are?"

"I don't know…six, maybe eight campfires spread out. No telling how many soldiers."

"They're pretty close to the co-op."

"Yeah," Bernie said, grimly. He met Luisa's eyes for a moment. She'd settled cross-legged into the dirt behind the crates with the five-year-old cradled in her lap.

Sweat dribbled down the dried mud on my arms and neck. "Is it safe to go *back* to the co-op?"

"How the fuck would I know that, Paula? Where else would we go?" Bernie raked his hands through his hair. He was sweating profusely.

"What if we went the long way around and tried to find the jeep?" I swatted a mosquito that landed on my neck.

"What long way around? You know a long way around?" He turned so that his back faced the crates, and then he sat with his legs straight out in front.

"Well, can we skirt around them without being seen?"

"I doubt it. They'll have sentries. As it is, we're damn lucky we didn't run into any on the trail. Just sit tight while we think through this."

The snatches of conversation suddenly pitched into the distinct sound of an argument.

I strained to see what was going on. "What are they saying?"

"I can't catch everything, but I think they're saying to cut the desalzado's throat, but away from camp because he'll attract flies." He got himself back into a squat and peeked through a slat.

"What's desalzado?"

"Paula, you need to learn some fucking Spanish! It's a forcibly recruited Contra. He was probably caught trying to escape."

Two men moved into the clearing. One pushed another, whose hands were tied behind his back, directly toward the crates. As they drew closer, I started to panic.

"They'll see us, Bernie."

He took firm hold of my arm. "Ssh."

When they were fifty feet from the crates, I saw that they were actually two boys, both dressed in camouflage and black rubber boots. The one in control looked older, maybe thirteen, fourteen. He had a puffy, sallow face, and the younger—no older than eleven—had features that echoed the other's, yet were so distorted by fear that his face appeared skull-like.

The older boy suddenly stopped, yanked the younger's head back by the hair, exposed his throat, and set the point of a knife against a throbbing vein. I studied his face, feeling as if my emotions were being forcibly concentrated in the pit of a crucible.

A breeze kicked up, and in the clearing a flap of tarpaulin inflated like a lung. Time slowed as it had during the last seconds of the accident. Again, I saw details with uncanny clarity—the downward crease at the corner of the older boy's mouth, the child's dark eyes, glazed by shock and disbelief, morbidly straining to see the knife tip. The older boy pricked the vein and a bead of blood ran the length of the blade.

The child whimpered, and still, the older boy hesitated. Was it to prolong the adrenaline rush of killing someone so personally or because the child's closeness made it harder? Blood pounded in my ears. Pressure built in my chest. And then I felt something shift, as if a tight knot of subcutaneous infection had risen to the surface.

A film moved across the older boy's eyes, and he slit the child's throat.

The air hummed. The barometric pressure increased so rapidly that I found it hard to breathe. A heat shimmer appeared and extended horizontally until I realized that it was agitating the garbage. That couldn't be right. I shook my head to clear my thoughts. There was no wind, but I could *see* it: the air vibrated as it danced around the boys. With each circuit, it began to extend vertically, pulling in leaves and clods of dirt, swirling around and around. The older boy, who had been staring at the twitching body of the child he'd just killed, looked up. For a moment, he seemed perplexed, and then his body went rigid. In the eerie quiet, the banana leaves had begun to ripple and bend, as if a giant hand swatted them back and forth. The air crackled with electricity.

The color drained from Bernie's face. In the clearing, the vibrating air had become a funnel, and it continued to enlarge. As it did, it sucked in more and more debris: chunks of concrete, rocks, tarpaulin, broken glass. It had reached twice the height of a man. I watched in disbelief as it slowly parodied a human form. A plastic sandal created the "O" of a mouth, arms took shape—independent swarms of refuse. A rum bottle stood like an erection. Finally, it lifted the dead child's body upward. His head lolled grotesquely, trailing blood, and yet, despite the vortex's violence, his limbs swam sleepily, as if he were trying to awaken from a dream. The older boy screamed. Contras ran from the jungle, discharging rifles and yelling in Spanish. Garbage and twigs flowed toward the older boy, then around him, crawled over him, animated him. His clothes filled until he appeared to bloat.

"*Do you see that?*" Bernie demanded.

Oh, yes, I saw it. Thousands of bits of debris spiraled faster and faster, and both boys were now caught like puppets within its midst. A stain spread down the older boy's pants leg as he loosed his bladder. Both boys had begun to move up the vortex.

Luisa silently sobbed, rocking back and forth with the five-year-old clutched to her. Bernie took deep shuddering breaths. I clawed at him, wishing that I could scream, anything to release the pressure in my chest. And then the sounds started, that cacophony of dissonance, and I knew what had visited me in the cave last night.

The soldiers stopped shooting. In the sudden quiet, all I could hear was the vortex's horrible mimicry of grief and terror and pain. I put my hands over my ears. I couldn't bear it. I looked to Luisa and Bernie. They couldn't hear those sounds. They would never hear them, nor would they ever feel the excruciating pain of it touching their mind.

A Contra raised the butt of his rifle and slammed it into the back of the soldier beside him. That man stumbled into the man in front of him, who turned, and then they all fell on each other hitting and stabbing. The vortex was as tall as the trees now. As the boys reached the top, its mouth opened. Their twisted bodies exploded into the surrounding trees, falling earthward in a series of crashes. Metal flew from the ground and began to slash like machetes across the dump. A rusted blade sliced one of the Contras neatly in half where he stood. Bernie squealed. He grabbed Luisa and the four of us fled.

In the co-op's dirt plaza, women washed the dead: ten boys and men, three women, one child. The little boy ran toward a sobbing teenage girl.

"¿Cómo te llamas?" Luisa called after him.

He paused. "Alberto," he said. Then the girl scooped him up and hugged him. Luisa went to the women in the plaza. Bernie and I headed for the kitchen fire and a bottle of rum. I rooted around for some cold beans and tortillas. After a few gulps of rum, he looked at me. "What the hell was that?" His eyes shone unnaturally bright.

I reached for the bottle. My mind was reeling. How could I explain to him the thoughts taking shape in my head? I wasn't sure I could explain them to myself. I took a swallow and felt the rum slide, hot and silky, into the bowl of my stomach. "If a flow of energy could wash life into the world…if that energy was violence…what do you think that life would look like?"

"You can't be serious!" He laughed. "That was a micro-burst. That was wind."

"Did you feel any wind when the debris swirled around the boys?"

"No, but…"

"Then tell me, Bernie, how did a microburst take on the features of a human face? How did a microburst grow arms to lift those little boys? What sliced that soldier in half with a machete?"

His eyes went wide and his voice had a high-pitched edge. "That's bullshit. It's not possible!"

Again I saw the bullet hole wavering, enlarging like a door being burnt open. I shuddered. I'd not yet looked through that door. The thought of doing so frightened me more than I could say. "Right now, Bernie, we need to focus on getting to Jinotega."

Again he seemed incredulous. "You're kidding me!"

"You have a better idea?" I handed the rum bottle back to him.

"Fuck, yeah! I say we go back to San Pedro and forget this shit."

I envisioned San Pedro's hydroelectric plant set into the hill below its penstock. I heard the turbine spinning, felt the water cold on my skin. And then I understood: the disruptions, the broken links, the warped sleeve, the fried bearings, all of it had occurred on the heels of violent clashes in the mountains nearby. The thing we'd seen thrived on violence. And once it fed, it roamed. Had it found the hydroelectric plant by accident? What was it, curious? Bored? My knees weakened.

"You think we'd be safe there, Bernie? It ever occur to you that whatever we saw out there might be what was messing with the hydroelectric plant in the first place?"

"Why fix the fucker then? Maybe if there's no hydroelectric plant there's nothing to draw whatever that was back to San Pedro!"

"You're not listening! The plant doesn't have anything to do with it. It's the fighting that draws it. What do you want us to do? Tell Luisa we're not going to fix the plant? To hell with putting lights in people's houses so that their children can do homework in the evenings? Fuck the vaccines, eh? Fuck them babies. We're goin' home."

I could see him struggle. His face flushed. His breath grew shallow. He turned from me as if caught in a private argument. He stepped forward and then back. Finally he nodded, and I realized how much both of our lives had come down to moral decisions that not even the need for self-preservation would allow us to abandon.

We cleaned up as best we could and then headed for the stashed jeep. As we removed its banana-leaf camouflage, the bearing sleeve glittered in the sunlight. I felt my consciousness superimposed onto the mountains that bordered Honduras. They loomed in the distance as a chain of unbroken conical ridges, successively higher and darker, purple-black and mottled as a deep bruise. A source of shelter, revolution, death... and life.

The edge of chaos.

"Are you all right, Paula?" Luisa asked. "You've blanched as white as a ghost."

Why did people always think that ghosts were white?

Bernie drove fast and didn't stop. I clung to the jeep's roll-bar with my teeth rattling in my head until I was sure they'd fall out. We passed charred vehicles lying in the weeds, lines of bullet holes along their sides. Bernie swerved like a maniac to avoid puddles. If the road was mined, they would be concealed in the puddles.

"Bernie, the road's not mined."

"How the *fuck* would you know that?"

He didn't look at me. He continued to swerve madly. I didn't say anything more. By mid-morning, we reached the machine shop, part of an electrical school with five students, about three miles from Jinotega. Bernie translated for me as I told the lead teacher—a latte-colored man named Roberto—what I needed. Roberto frowned at the sleeve but said, "Sí, Sí. La tienda puede hacerlo. Mis alumnos son los mejores."

"What's he saying?"

"He says the shop can handle it. His students are the best."

"Ask him if he's heard of a man named Rafael Fuentes."

"Sí, he escuchado sobre él. La gente lo llama el loco local. Tiene un bungalow en el Lago de Apanás. Si toma el camino que va hacia el norte desde Jinotega, lo encontrará."

"They call him the local nutcase. He has a bungalow on Lake Apanás. If you follow the road that goes north from Jinotega, you'll find it. Why? Who is he?"

"A friend of a friend."

We headed into town for some food while the machinists worked. Jinotega materialized one purple-and-rose-colored shack at a time. Government militia encamped in the central plaza, their headquarters surrounded by barbed wire, trenches and sandbags. Several .50 caliber machine guns and a large, turreted, anti-aircraft gun pointed northwest toward Honduras. Soldiers in camouflage, with floppy hats shielding their eyes, walked the streets, cradling rifles.

We stopped at the first café we saw, Paolo's, an open one-story cement building painted in orange and green. We ordered coffee, black beans and tortillas. The coffee smelled of chicory. It moved me to tenderness to listen to Bernie and Luisa weave a future in complete denial of what I had begun to fear we faced.

"Once the hydro plant is fixed, I'd fancy a do to celebrate," Luisa said. "Félix's cousins have a Mariachi band. Get our knees up a bit. Why don't we buy a few pints while we're here to take back and store in the refrigerator, eh?"

"A party with cold beer and dancing—sounds good," Bernie agreed.

The food came out. I watched the two of them enjoying each other, bantering back and forth about the possible party. All the while, I felt pressure building: an underlying vibration, like I experienced at the hydro plant when turbulence built in the penstock. Absently, I began to massage the tightness in my chest.

"How did you end up in a place like San Pedro, Paula?" Bernie asked.

The unexpected question startled me. I stared at him… and then I was reliving it:

I had found Jorge Ramírez's house in Barrio Riguero and knocked on the door. It opened, revealing a woman with dark circles under her eyes and a thick streak of gray running through her brown hair. On her hip she balanced a sickly looking little girl. Quizzically the woman looked me up and down. When she spotted the pistol in my hand, she blanched.

I pushed myself through the door. "Where's Jorge?"

He was in the kitchen kneeling behind an overturned chair, apparently trying to fix a hole in its woven seat. The room smelled strongly of onions. A pot bubbled on the wood stove and the rickety kitchen table had been set with chipped dishes. The ordinariness of the domestic scene diminished Jorge in my eyes. What had I expected to find: evil itself laughing maniacally? For a moment I felt uncertain about the entire issue of justice.

The woman put the child down and stepped in front of her. Jorge rose and with him my rage once again engulfed me. "Don't hurt us!" he pleaded.

"Why not? Because you have a child? You bastard, you killed Mercedes!"

I raised the pistol and pointed it at the woman's head. "How would you like me to take what you love?"

The woman's face twisted in fear. The child began to scream.

"Shut up. Shut her up!" I yelled.

"I tell them times only. Locations. Where she speaks, who she meets with. They say they just want to keep track of her. No one ever say anything about killing."

"What did you get in return, Jorge? Privileges? Extra food? Money?" I cocked the pistol and the sound was like an alarm waking me from a dream. I stared at the gun in my hand and a cold terror froze my insides. What was I doing? Threatening an

innocent woman? What was I going to do? Kill her? Me? I was capable of that?

"The girl is sick. They promise me she can go to a doctor in Texas."

For a moment I fantasized dragging Jorge into the plaza, exposing his betrayal and then helping the crowd beat him to death. But the moment had passed. The gun had grown heavy in my hand. I couldn't kill to sate my anger. I wouldn't. I let out a low cry, spun on my heel and slammed the door behind me.

I couldn't comprehend what Jorge'd done in the same way that I couldn't comprehend Mercedes' murder. The incident kept throwing itself at me night after night.

I'd believed we were protected. I'd never consciously thought such a thing, but I'd believed it. We were smart, educated, sincere…American. Weren't those all the ingredients of a protection spell? The depth of my own naiveté stunned me.

After the incident in Barrio Riguero, the thought of going back to INE and possibly running into Jorge Ramírez was unbearable. I'd already made the decision not to return to the States, and so I had begged Simon to transfer me from the geothermal project. They needed someone to work on hydroelectric in San Pedro. But Bernie and Luisa didn't know about Mercedes.

"You okay, Luv?" Luisa asked, covering my hand with her own. "You look a million miles away."

"What?" They were both looking at me with some concern. "Sorry. I don't know, Bernie. It was never a plan. It just kind of happened. How about you?"

"Me? I got it into my head that I wanted to write a novel set in the jungles of Central America. I guess I thought I'd write *The Heart of Darkness* and slip it past my editor in the guise of a romance." He laughed so loudly that several heads turned in our direction. "America tells the world that it's fighting for democracy for poor Mestizos when in reality it's enabling the kidnap of eleven-year-olds—" his voice quavered. The horror of the child's murder still gripped us. He grasped Luisa's hand, brought her fingers to his lips and kissed them.

"Why write romances if you feel that strongly?"

"Because I'm afraid I'll flinch." He squeezed Luisa's hand. "I'll intend to tell the truth and then I won't. I'll start to pretty things up. The world will start to look the way I want it to look rather than the way that it is." He shook his head. "No one takes you seriously if you flinch. I'm better off writing fluff where the world's ugliness is conquerable, love prevails, and everything works out happily ever after. They're very popular, and I can churn out one of those puppies every three months."

Paolo stopped by and offered more coffee. As he refilled my cup, the café shuddered so violently that dust fell from the rafters. He staggered backward, splashing coffee onto the floor. The air smelled acrid. We ran into the street, unsure of what was happening. Soldiers swarmed toward the plaza from the northwest, shooting machine guns and rocket-propelled grenades.

"¡Somos los cachorros de Reagan!"

Another pounding concussion...Paolo dropped the coffee pot and the four of us dove for cover behind a water tank beside the café. In the plaza soldiers scrambled to return fire, shooting off bursts from their AK-47s and then diving for cover.

I heard a rhythmic thudding and looked up. Two Soviet-built Mi-24 helicopters swooped in from the south, their bellies just skimming the treetops. I'd heard that the Sandinistas had acquired these. Their paths split. One headed northeast toward lake Apanás, while the other barreled toward the central plaza, its turret guns sweeping the side streets. So many bullets discharged, kicking up mud and chipping the concrete bases of the buildings, that they created a visible wave of noise.

The chopper paused above the plaza, its churning blades drawing up muddy air until an opaque column wavered independently above the cobbles. My heart stalled in my chest as I watched that column grow, gaining energy as the fighting escalated. It began to move, ripping sheets of corrugated metal from rooftops, snatching bicycles from doorways, uprooting trees…clothing itself in the materials at hand.

The pressure rose until it constricted my chest. My head filled with a cacophony of dissonance. A face of smoke and fire, assembled from burning tires, rotated toward me as if its conceit of eyes had actually conferred sight. I trembled, gagged on the smell of torched rubber. I felt it searching… and then it was flaying into me. Pain exploded inside my head. For a moment the pain was so intense that the view darkened. In the blackness, the bullet hole wavered, and then gradually enlarged. For the first time, I inched toward that door and looked through. Beyond its threshold spun a vortex. I fell to my knees and vomited into the dirt.

An arm, shaped of debris, separated itself from the column and grasped one of the chopper's rotating blades. With a grinding screech, the chopper went down. In the plaza, soldiers swiveled machine guns in order to fire. Contras and Sandinistas were brutalizing each other in hand-to-hand combat. When the vortex lost interest in the smashed chopper it spun the anti-aircraft gun's turret like a child's toy.

"Bernie, we need to move!"

He clung to Luisa. They'd lodged themselves in a cubby created by the water tank butting up against the café wall. He looked as if he didn't recognize me. I shook him and motioned in the direction of the jeep. His eyes focused momentarily. He got to his feet. I tried to rouse Paolo but he had glued himself to the café wall and refused to budge.

"Give me the keys, Bernie! You can't drive!"

I pushed him and Luisa into the jeep's back seat and then jumped behind the wheel. Framed in the windshield, the vortex turned its hellish stare on me. Shaking, I twisted the key in the ignition, tried to jam the gearshift into reverse, missed, and stalled the engine. The creature broke off one of the chopper's blades and sent it whirling. Again I twisted the key. The engine caught and whined, wheels spinning in the muck. I ground into reverse and swung the jeep around. The chopper blade gouged into the mud close enough to cover us in a thick spray.

The helicopter that had ventured toward the lake returned and opened fire. I hunched over the wheel, jammed the gear-shift into first and spun east. Behind me a roar built until the ground itself shook. I swerved through a rickety fence, across a squalid back yard nearly opaqued by smoke and onto the next street and the next, careening around corners until an overturned military truck materialized in our path.

A pillar of smoke and fire had risen above the rooftops. I reversed, headed west, sped down side streets for four blocks—then another impasse: an anti-aircraft gun crumpled like a piece of paper across the road.

My only option was to go east again. Unexpectedly, the central plaza reappeared to my left. I slammed on the brakes. Bernie flew partway into the front seat.

I was being forced to circle a single point, to repeat an elliptical path…like Jupiter's eye…like the boys caught in the vortex…like….

I needed to talk to Fuentes.

"What are you doing?" Bernie gasped, trying to regain his breath. At least his wits were returning.

"Bernie, Fuentes is no more than ten minutes from here. He knows more about chaos and complexity than anyone else on the planet. I have to talk to him!"

A volley of bullets dug into the ground directly in front of the jeep. The driver's-side headlight shattered. "Shit!" As I slammed into reverse, a bullet pinged off the fender.

"Luisa and I know the road to the lake. We've been there before," Bernie said. Luisa squeezed his shoulder.

"What about Contras?"

"That helicopter swept back pretty fast. Could mean it didn't find anything to engage," Luisa said. Still, she took a magazine clip from the pouch, slipped it into the AK-47's mag well and locked it into place.

"You know how to use that thing?"

"Unfortunately, yes. Don't shilly-shally, Luv. Let's move."

Two more helicopters barreled in from the south. As the vortex slid toward them, I felt its attention drift and with it the pain in my head lessened.

I headed north at top speed.

Fuentes' house rested on pilings two feet aboveground. We careened into his yard amidst a flurry of feathers and clucking as unhappy chickens fled beneath the steps. The front door opened and a man emerged bare-footed, wearing jeans and a T-shirt. He had a rifle trained on us. It surprised me how tall he was, at least 6'1", much taller than most Nicaraguans. He was lean-limbed, with cinnamon-colored skin and surprisingly curly, dark hair.

"Escuchamos disparos. ¿Los Contras han atacado?" He could see the smoke billowing above Jinotega, and he was close enough to have heard the rocket launchers.

"¡Sí, los Contras atacaron!" Bernie confirmed.

"Do you speak English?" I asked.

"Yes, what do you want?"

"My name is Paula Hunter. I'm looking for Rafael Fuentes."

"Why are you looking for him? Who are you?"

"Mercedes Zapatera was my closest friend."

"Ah." He exhaled sharply and then shook his head as if to control his emotions. He pointed the barrel of the gun toward the ground. "Yes, I remember. We were to meet in Boaco." He stepped forward, grasped my hand and then put the gun down so he could embrace me with his other arm, pounding me firmly on the back three times. He smelled of tobacco. When he released me, I saw that his eyes were hazel.

I introduced Luisa and Bernie. He embraced them as well.

"Please, come in. Were soldiers on the road?"

"No, we didn't have any trouble," I said, as I climbed the steps.

"That doesn't mean we're safe, but hopefully it gives us some breathing room," Bernie added.

Inside, the house was sparse but comfortable, its one striking feature a glassless window that overlooked the lake.

Large wormwood shutters allowed him to close off the space if the weather grew cool. In the window's light sat a comfortable-looking chair with books stacked on the floor as high as its arm rests.

"Sit." Fuentes motioned to a roughly hewn kitchen table surrounded by a mismatch of chairs and stools. A kerosene lantern hung above it.

After he'd brought water, he sat with us. "Drink, the water is potable." He took out a tobacco pouch and began to roll a cigarette. "I wanted to warn Mercedes that her politics put her in danger. I left Managua because I was constantly followed; everywhere there were little ears, little eyes. I was afraid. At first I didn't contact her because..." he trailed off. He didn't have to say it. He'd been hoping to drop off the Contras' radar screen and contacting Mercedes would have been a bright-red and noisy blip. "...but then I heard something and my conscience.... I hoped that, once in Boaco, I could convince her not to go back to Managua.

"I have a boat. I can take you across the lake. Will this help?"

Luisa, Bernie, and I looked at each other. He thought we needed help to escape the Contras.

"Dr. Fuentes—"

"Call me Rafi." He lit the cigarette and inhaled.

"Rafi, we're here to discuss your work on the emergence of complex systems. It appears to have posed one hell of an ontological question."

He startled. "What are you talking about?"

"Mercedes once suggested to me that violence itself might create bifurcation points. It's a feedback loop, right? The output of one act is fed back in as input for the next..." For a horrific moment I was standing again in Jorge's kitchen with a gun pointed at his wife's head. I shivered. "In a war so much energy is being amplified..."

Rafi choked on his cigarette smoke and coughed. "An adaptive system? Are you crazy?"

"You said yourself that outcomes don't just happen; they build up gradually as small chance events become magnified by feedback. When we were traveling to Boaco, Mercedes said you were working on the equations to show how randomness can select one equilibrium point to create an isolated self-sustained energy."

"Yes, a soliton like Jupiter's eye. Not a sentient being!"

"But those same forces of self-organization and emergence apply to the creation of living systems just as surely as they do to Jupiter's eye!"

Luisa and Bernie were silent. Fuentes stood up from the table. He began to pace and to mutter under his breath in Spanish.

"I understand that it's difficult to accept but I know—do you hear me—I know that this impossible thing has happened. I...I have a sensitivity. It happened the night Mercedes was murdered. I hit my head pretty hard when our car rolled. When I saw the bullet hole in the passenger window, I knew she was dead. I felt pain so intense that I momentarily lost my ability to see.

"The bullet hole began to waver and enlarge, eating outward as if it were a door opening. Every circuit in my body ignited. Afterward, I began experiencing moments of intuition that would gradually build to clarity, as if a light had switched on in the recesses of my brain, illuminating a previously unexplored path. I would know things. I wouldn't know how or why, but I would know them with certainty.

"When I moved to San Pedro, I began to feel a presence in the jungle. It seemed to come on the heel of violent skirmishes, but I didn't put two and two together for awhile. It was mucking with the hydroelectric plant, but I'm not sure why. Maybe it came across the plant while roaming. Maybe it was curious. Maybe it was playing. I don't know.

"I didn't see it feeding off of the attack at the cooperative, but it was there, in the jungle that night. It approached me while we were in the cave." I swallowed. "And when that happened, it was able to make me understand, on a primitive level, what it perceived."

All three of them looked at me as if I'd just said that I'd recently arrived from Mars.

"It spoke to you?" Fuentes said, incredulous.

Bernie fidgeted. "I thought you'd seriously lost it. Luisa and I couldn't hear it or feel it. We weren't able to see it either until the debris it sucked in at the dump gave it shape. You're the only one who can, aren't you?"

"Yes."

"Bloody Hell," Luisa cursed.

"Why Nicaragua? Why now?"

I shrugged. "Happenstance." Though who was to say that it hadn't happened before or wouldn't again? There were plenty of hot spots in the world. Places trapped in their own unending turbulence.

"Can we dissipate it, Rafi? It not only feeds off the violence. I believe it intensifies it."

"If such a thing existed, it would maintain and propagate crudely. When the violence stopped, it would die."

Luisa laughed. "Right, then, let's tell the Contras and Sandinistas that they have to stop fighting."

"What if it can migrate to feed? It moved easily between San Pedro and Jinotega. What if it can move from conflict to conflict, traveling the length of Central and South America from Honduras to Argentina? What happens then?" Bernie demanded.

I put my hand across my heart. Pressure was building in my chest.

Rafi watched the smoke from his cigarette rise into sudden eddies. "No, in chaotic systems, there is always an attractor at the heart of the chaos. It's a point that the equations converge on. Always." He squinted toward the lake.

I followed his gaze. Outside, water rose in random spouts, murky microbursts colored by disturbed sediment. A breeze wafted through the window, and I caught the scent of torched rubber. My heart shuddered. Slowly, the microbursts resolved themselves into a triplet of spirals. They circled, dipping toward shore and then away in an otherworldly waltz. Like vines intertwining, they gradually merged into a single water spout: tall, stationary, dark. Muddy limbs blossomed with the parasitic beauty of orchids. Water reeds and grasses weaved themselves through the funnel and into the features of a vacant face. Why did it parody us? But then…why wouldn't it? We had given it birth. We fed it with our murder and brutality. Who else would it mimic?

As the face rotated toward shore, the funnel began to move.

Rafi and Bernie raced to close and brace the shutters. Luisa ran to the front door and latched it, as if such a thing might help!

I did not have to see the vortex's approach. I felt immersed long before water careened into Fuentes' tin roof and bled into the house around the shutter seams. It prowled the outside walls, mauled the pilings and flung itself against the wood siding until the house groaned. A dog yelped suddenly and then went silent.

Rafi winced. He got up and came to stand behind me. He put his hands on my shoulders and bent close to my ear. "Does it speak?"

I felt the warmth of his breath against my cheek. "No." Water hissed at the floor boards and slithered adder-tongued between my toes.

Rafi whispered, "Maybe you should try?"

Me? I closed my eyes and listened to it surge beneath the house. I'd devoted my life to the rational and analytical and yet here I found myself in a world without sense. With a tendril of fear, I probed the door that had been burnt into darkness. Pain, brilliant and blinding in its acuteness, pounded my forehead, my eyes, my jaw It was too much.

"I can't do it!" I gasped. In my lap, my hands had turned ashen. Shaking, I got up from the table and stumbled toward the chair in front of the wormwood shutters. Rafi didn't move.

Luisa rested her head on Bernie's chest, stoic, resigned. Bernie held her like a treasure.

"I understand fear!" Rafi said. He raked his hand into his dark curls and grasped several in a fist. "But, if you can communicate with it, knowing what we need to do may be easier, yes?"

"He's right, Paula," Bernie choked out.

"That hole in the darkness where you want me to go is a place of pain, both physical and emotional. It's a place where an impossible thing exists. There is no reason that I can apply. I…I can't…." I buried my face in my hands. What if I lost my way in the pain? Would the vortex trap me in an inescapable loop of agony? And what if I did nothing? Who did I doom? The four of us? Jinotega? Nicaragua?

I looked up and saw Luisa's eyes burning with such compassion that I thought my heart would break. She came to me and gently smoothed the hair from my face. Then she took both my hands in hers and held them firmly. Such a simple act and yet my gratitude overwhelmed me. She'd offered herself as an anchor.

I returned her grip and willed myself to stop shaking.

"I'm afraid, Luisa. I don't know what will happen."

"Shush, Luv. I know."

"No, I mean it could be just as dangerous for you as it is for me to approach the vortex."

"You have to try, Paula. I won't let go no matter what. Promise."

I closed my eyes, focused my breath, and again approached the hole burnt into darkness. At its threshold I grasped Luisa's hands even tighter, and then I stepped into the unknown, past the smell of burning rubber, into an eclipse so dense and close I thought I would suffocate. The pain in my head danced like solar flares. I told myself that Luisa was my Ariadne's thread. As long as I held her hands, I would find my way back from the scorch of mind-searing pain, this blindness of light.

It thrived…. And why not? It felt no guilt or misgiving. It was not bothered by questions of right or wrong, of mercy or justice. There was only the energy upon which it fed and the strange attraction that...that....

The pain intensified. It flayed me open, cracked me to my core, left me alone and empty. I'd been wrong about the hydroelectric plant. It wasn't a coincidence. It had sensed me, just as I'd sensed it. The door that had opened the night of the accident had been opened by an act of violence, just as violence had given the vortex life. In some inexplicable way I had become the attractor around which its butterfly wings had formed. It might have been born from atrocities committed in the mountains, but it was me it had followed to La Suprema. Me it had followed to Jinotega. Me it had followed to Fuentes. *It was me.* My entire being rebelled. In my mind, I turned and fled.

When I opened my eyes I had Luisa's hands in a death grip. The first thing I noticed was how hot she was, burning as if with fever. I let go of her hands and she slumped against me. Bernie, glassy-eyed and flushed, ran to her limp form.

"Luisa!" He held his hand in front of her nose and mouth. "God, she's not breathing!" He tipped back her head, pinched her nose and started forcing breath into her lungs. Rafi hurried over and knelt beside her, pressing his fingers against her wrist. For a moment he seemed perplexed, and then, with a jolt, his expressive face looked at me with both despair and disbelief. "I can't find her pulse."

"No," Bernie said, firmly. "No. That's not possible." Again he tipped her head back and forced air into her lungs.

Another minute went by. Bernie gasped for breath, his face beet-colored. His eyes were terrible to see, wild, desperate, an animal with its leg mangled in a trap. Rafi held his ear to her chest, felt her neck for a pulse, checked for respiration. He gave me an almost imperceptible head shake. *No.*

This couldn't be happening. I slid out of the chair, knocking over the stacked books.

"Bernie," Rafi said gently, laying a hand on his arm. Bernie shoved him away. He pulled Luisa to his chest and buried his face in her hair.

Bernie grew eerily calm with Luisa's death. It frightened me more than if he were screaming and raving. I feared he was in the eye of a great storm. He carried her body to Rafi's bedroom off the kitchen.

When he returned we sat at the table. All my energy was directed at not breaking down. I felt completely numb as I explained what I'd discovered. Afterward I said, "I think I can lead it away from the fighting. I can't control it, but I'm pretty sure I define a boundary for it. I think it has to follow me…eventually."

Bernie's struggle was terrible to see. We waited in silence as he visibly pulled himself together. Eventually he cleared his throat, but I couldn't face the desperation in his eyes. I had to turn away as he spoke. "You don't know what its range is, or how often it has to feed or how long it can survive." And then his words became so cold and steady that they felt like blows. "With your luck it's like a goddamned tortoise that can go six months without food or water! What if it realizes what you're trying to do? What keeps it from killing you and moving on?"

"No, Bernie, I've got a hunch. I feel a sudden increase in pressure when it's close."

"So?"

"It's cyclone season in the Caribbean."

Rafi arched an eyebrow. "An intense low pressure system."

"Exactly. I have a strong feeling that the vortex hasn't reached its full potential yet. If I can get it into the Caribbean, the pressure differentials within a good storm might tear it apart."

"That's a lot of ifs."

"Jesus, Bernie, I have to try! Besides this isn't your worry. I won't let Luisa die in vain. You're going to get that sleeve back to San Pedro. Oscar knows enough that he might be able to get the plant on line until someone from INE can replace me.

I don't care what it takes. You get those vaccines distributed. You do that for her."

He broke down completely.

You're taking a terrible risk, Luv, Luisa whispered inside my head. I paused. I could feel her presence, insubstantial, barely more than a fading susurration. Was this a new aspect of my sensitivity? I shook my head as if to clear it, closed my eyes. *But, you have to try.* I opened my eyes. A dissolving hand faded from Bernie's arm.

"Listen," Rafi said, cocking his head.

"What?"

He went to the wormwood shutters and placed an ear against them. "It's quiet." Then he unbolted and opened them.

The vortex had retreated.

Slowly, I went to Bernie and put my hand on his shoulder. "We need to bury Luisa."

"I don't want you to lead that thing away, Paula. I want you to kill that son-of-a-bitch. I want you to make it squeal with pain. You understand me?" Bernie said.

Once more I was standing in Jorge's kitchen with a gun pointed at his wife's head. I squeezed Bernie's shoulder. I understood.

After we buried Luisa, we brought the radio inside and tried to pick up news from Jinotega. None of us expected the fighting to come to the lake but it would be foolhardy not to prepare. We decided to take four-hour shifts watching the road. Rafi got his boat ready. If we spotted soldiers, the best thing to do would be to head across the lake. But I was already thinking past that.

"Could we take the boat from the lake into Rio Tuma?" I asked.

He shook his head, no. "You can't get into the Tuma from the lake. Besides it isn't navigable until it flows into the Rio Grande de Matagalpa."

That was about fifty miles from the Caribbean. My hope had been to take the boat from the lake into the river and follow the river until it emptied into the ocean. It was problematic not being able to take Rafi's boat. That meant I'd have to take the road when it opened. It was at least sixty miles to Mulukuku, the tiny town on the banks of the river where the Tuma emptied into the Rio Grande. If I was lucky and didn't run into a road block, land mine or downpour that made the road impassable, I could do it in five or six hours. If not, I'd be spending a night in the lowlands. Less chance of running into Contras and Sandinistas—I'd be moving away from the fighting. But moving out of the mountains into the lowlands had its problems, too. The climate was tropical and with heat came bot flies, dengue fever, lethal kissing beetles, scorpions and rats. And when I got to Mulukuku, I'd still have to get a boat. How I was going to do that, I had no idea. It wasn't like I just happened to be carrying a wad of Cordoba.

Rafi started going through his cabinets: Rice, sugar, oil, coffee. Not much. Maybe not enough food to survive. Not enough money to get a boat…. I forced those thoughts out of my mind as best I could.

"Rafi, Bernie needs to get that sleeve back to San Pedro. Can he borrow your truck?"

"You can't be serious. You're not going alone," Bernie protested. "You don't know the language!"

"He's right, Paula. You can't go alone, at the very least you need someone riding shotgun," Rafi said.

"I'm going," Bernie said. "We started this together. We'll finish it that way."

"But the sleeve!"

"That's something I could do," Rafi said. "I have this skill. I could take the sleeve back to San Pedro and help Oscar get the plant back on line."

"Can you handle the AK-47, Bernie?"

"Of course I can," he said. I hoped he wasn't lying.

"Well, I guess that means I'm driving."

Still, it was two days before we picked up news on the shortwave that the road was safe. During that time I slept when I wasn't on watch. I bathed in the lake and gathered eggs from the chickens. We ate scrambled eggs with rice and mangoes. We drank coffee at the kitchen table with the breeze coming in through the open window. Rafi read books. When Bernie wasn't on watch, he spent his time sitting next to Luisa's grave.

Rafi gave us one of his chickens. "She's a good layer. Usually an egg a day. And if it comes to it, she'll make a good stew."

"Thanks, Rafi."

He measured out what other staples he could spare. We left in the morning of the third day. I put the chicken in a flour sack with a hole cut in it so she could stick her head out, and then I settled her in the back seat. She pecked at the upholstery and made pleasant conversation with herself. I don't know why that made me feel better, but it did.

Jinotega looked just like you'd think it would after a fierce battle: devastated buildings, burnt vehicles, people wandering around with shocked and vacant faces. I scanned the road in every direction looking for signs of the vortex. By the time we were a half hour south of town, my nerves were taut enough to break.

"Where is it?" Bernie demanded, his face grave. "What if it doesn't follow! What if this doesn't work!"

"It'll follow." The thing I didn't know was whether I'd be able to come back from another encounter. Luisa had died anchoring me. I'd have to go through that door alone next time. Would it rip me apart before I could lure it into a storm? And what if Bernie was right? What if removed from its feeding ground it was able to go dormant like a spore, rather than dispersing? What if the storm front pushed it inland rather than the pressure differentials destroying it? What if—

Bernie reached over and squeezed my shoulder. "How long will it take us to reach Mulukuku?"

"Depends. I'm more worried about obtaining a boat once we get there."

"No worries. I'll offer them signed first editions of all my books. Nicaraguans love romances."

I wrinkled my nose. "What?"

He winked. "We'll trade the jeep and the gun for a boat. God knows we won't need either in the Caribbean."

I blushed. "Why didn't I think of that?"

"I don't know. Maybe you had other things on your mind. We're not coming back from this, are we?"

I didn't say anything. I didn't see how we could.

He nodded. He picked up the AK-47, inserted a clip into the mag well, and then checked the chamber to make sure there was a round ready to go. He went back to watching the road. An hour past Jinotega we turned east. Half way to Mulukuku it started to rain. By two thirds of the way, it was pouring. The road turned to mud, and we slowed to a crawl. We didn't bother to check the depth of flash streams this time. We just engaged the four wheel drive and kept moving. The chicken didn't like the rain. She started to complain so loudly that Bernie finally fished her from the back seat and settled her on his lap. She calmed down almost instantly. I was watching him unconsciously gentle her when the jeep suddenly canted left in the flash stream we were crossing and stopped dead. I down shifted. The tires spun in the mud. We were caught on something. So much for getting to Mulukuku by nightfall. I got out to see how bad it was. A fairly large tree limb had lodged between the front wheels. The wind had risen, and I heard a deep rumbling of thunder.

"Bernie get the saw out of the back, will you?"

The pouring rain made it hard to see. The limb itself was below water. Bernie started working through it. Lightning flashed. The saw blade slipped. My body felt distanced as Bernie's hand came out of the water, and I watched the blood flow. I got him into the back seat of the jeep and rummaged in my pack for the soap and chamois. He'd perched the chicken on the console between the bucket seats when he'd gotten out of the jeep. She cocked her head and clucked.

We were soaked to the skin. I dried my face and then cleaned the wound. The blade had sliced into the soft tissue between his thumb and forefinger severing the muscle.

I couldn't do much about the muscle, but the wound would have to be stitched to keep him from bleeding to death. I didn't have anything for pain. I got out a sewing needle and dental floss from the haphazard medical kit and sterilized the needle in the flame of a waterproof match.

He was very pale. "Don't you dare go into shock on me, Bernie."

"You sewed as a girl, right?" he said, watching me make two unsuccessful attempts at threading the needle.

"Made all my own clothes," I lied. With trembling hands I went to work. At least he had the good sense to pass out before I swabbed the wound with tincture of iodine and wrapped it with gauze.

Ominous clouds pressed in, scraping like a low-slung belly through the trees. The lightning and thunder intensified. I closed my eyes and leaned my head against the seat. The wind had begun to rock the jeep. This was more than rainy season downpour. There was a storm moving in.

"Bernie? Bernie, can you hear me?"

"Luisa?" He opened his eyes. I could see his confusion. What was Paula doing in his room? Where was Luisa? He started to sit up and winced in pain. I watched it all come flooding back. He wasn't in his room…Luisa was…. He was in a stalled jeep…it was still raining. He looked to me. "What are we even doing here?"

"We're here for the same reason we took that sleeve to Jinotega. Because we both found something that mattered to us, and we thought we could make a difference. We've got to get out, Bernie. Keep going. If it keeps raining like this the jeep will be underwater in another couple of hours."

"Where we walking to?"

"There's a banana plantation outside Mulukuku. It'll have a concrete bunker. If we can get out of the stream, then, with just a little bit of luck, we'll be able to find shelter."

He watched the wind battering everything in view. It was probably twenty-five, thirty miles an hour already and quickly rising. I didn't know how close the banana plantation outside Mulukuku was. One mile? Five? Again the jeep rocked.

"We'll never make it, Paula," he said, gently. He took my hand. "We made a good try."

In the end, I supposed that's all anyone could do.

The jeep shuddered and shifted. I felt the limb scrape the underside of the suspension and then, it was past us. I shoved the chicken aside and scrambled into the driver's seat to re-engage the engine. Very slowly I eased the jeep out of the flash stream and onto higher ground. As I lurched forward with a renewed surge of hope, my head filled with a cacophony of dissonance.

"Hang on back there." I stepped on the gas and headed into the wind.

I sensed the vortex reaching toward my sensitivity with its needle-sharp talons. The wind howled. Lightning hit. On either side of the road, a tangle of trees and vines strobed forth before falling again into the blur of rain. Ahead, the muscle of the wind boomed and a palm bent so far backward that it snapped and then twirled through the air like a baton. *Please, just let my luck last a little longer, please, please.* The storm churned down, the wind rising faster and faster. The jeep blew sideways like a leaf. I gritted my teeth, swung the wheel hard to correct, and kept going.

Suddenly the jeep lifted and spun. I couldn't tell if it was a wind surge from the storm or if the vortex had thrown us. We hurtled into the trees, our headlights illuminating an undecipherable confusion of leaves and vines. We lodged in the fork of two massive old-growth Mahogany trees. The impact smashed the driver's side door and knocked the wind out of me. I felt pain radiate down my left side. Bernie had crumpled on the floor of the back seat. The wind had grown too loud for me to call to him. I didn't know if he was conscious or even alive. The jeep groaned and shuddered, but by some miracle the trees held us and protected us from the worst of the increasing wind. I tried to slide from behind the wheel but pain rooted me in place. I hunkered down as best I could and clutched the chicken. She was terrified, struggling to get out of her sack. The impulse to flee, to escape was so strong.

The vortex swam around me. I could feel it struggling. Its counter-clockwise rotation faltered. It tried to reform horizontally to reduce its height. I closed my eyes and approached the door that had opened with Mercedes' murder. I'd never thought of grief as a combustible material before or that there might be a revelatory nature to pain, but my fear had been burned away. I felt compressed, purified, as if I'd been winnowed down to something simple and clean.

The chicken relaxed against me. I was singing to her, I think. She couldn't hear me. I couldn't hear myself, but it was my euphony pitted against the vortex's dissonance. I stepped into the mind-numbing pain with the calm of a hurricane's eye, a point of stability in a crucible of turbulence. I was at peace.

The vortex couldn't feed off of the storm. It seemed perplexed, frustrated at the world into which it had been born and isolated. It was to me that it whispered its loss, perhaps in sympathy to my own. Again it faltered. It was being blown asunder. The dissonant sounds it bombarded me with turned plaintive. It uprooted a palm and tossed it at the storm. The impulse to lash back at what has hurt you was so strong.

I grasped for mind holds like hand and foot holds. This was closure for both of us. A scream of terror erupted inside my head and then there was silence. It was gone. But I knew that, under the right circumstances, another like it could manifest. I felt neither joy nor triumph.

Some workers from the banana plantation outside of Mulukuku found us the next day. I passed out when they pulled me from behind the steering wheel. Apparently, I had several cracked ribs and a broken arm.

I awoke flat on my back on a bunk at the plantation. Bernie was sitting beside me. He had a bandage across his forehead and one of his eyes was swollen shut.

"Boy, do you look like crap," I said.

"Yeah, I like you, too. How's the arm?"

I looked at it. Someone had bound it with duct tape between two planks of wood. Jungle medicine. I felt my ribs. They'd duct-taped those, too. Ow. I wasn't going anywhere soon.

Bernie cleared his throat. "I…I'm not going back to San Pedro, Paula."

Luisa. I understood. "What are you going to do?"

He looked into the distance. "Back to the states, I think. I have an idea for a new book."

"A romance?"

He smiled. "No, a fantasy. Here's my opening paragraph: Dragons are sensitive to pressure, both within the earth and within people, and so they are unavoidably drawn to places of great upheaval and to people possessed of great passion. Perhaps they sense that such pressure, if it does not crush, will compress raw material into its purified form. It is this compressed and rarefied beauty they admire, and so they hoard jewels. But so too are they attracted to people slowly compressed and purified by the events of their lives."

I heard a cluck.

"Ah, I see you have another visitor." He reached down and picked up the chicken and settled her beside me.

I laughed. Ouch. The ribs. "I should name her."

"What about Tiamat?" he said.

"The embodiment of chaos and mother of the first gods? Isn't that a lot of baggage for a chicken?"

He chuckled. "Where are you headed when you can travel?"

I thought for a moment. "Back to San Pedro. Maybe try to expand hydroelectric power to other villages." I could see he was surprised. I was a little surprised myself. Was I really willing to risk that it could happen again? That at some unpredictable moment the right concentration of brutality and terror might create another vortex and my sensitivity act as its attractor? The truth was that putting electricity in people's homes had grown to matter to me. For the first time that I could remember, I had a reason to go somewhere. A reason to stay. Yes, I would risk it.

Bernie cleared his throat. "Anyway, I just wanted to say good-bye. The transport truck will be heading out shortly. I talked to the foreman. He'll see you get to wherever you need to go when you're up to traveling." He stood.

"I think you got it right about the dragons."

"Thanks." He kissed my forehead and left.

I never saw Bernie again. Eventually, Tiamat and I went back to San Pedro and got to work teaching Oscar and Rigalo and Miguelito how to use a voltmeter, how to measure current, how to install light bulbs, how to run wire. With enough work, one day they would wire houses for electricity themselves.

More Nancy Kress at Phoenix Pick

ACT ONE
AI UNBOUND
THE BODY HUMAN

www.PhoenixPick.com

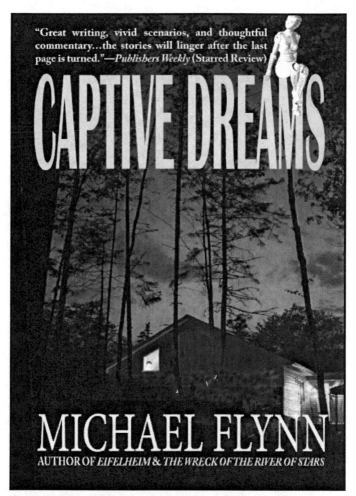

CAPTIVE DREAMS

MICHAEL FLYNN

AUTHOR OF *EIFELHEIM* & *THE WRECK OF THE RIVER OF STARS*

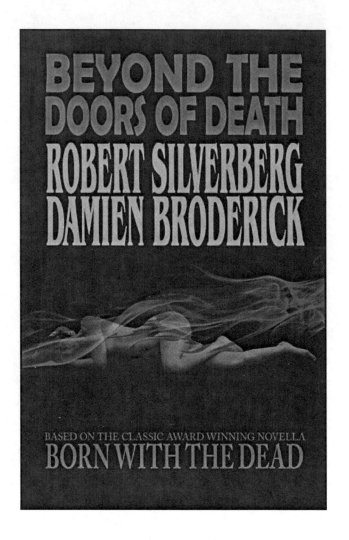

BASED ON THE CLASSIC AWARD WINNING NOVELLA
BORN WITH THE DEAD

"Broad, intriguing speculation on human evolution and first contact."
—*Publishers Weekly*

www.PhoenixPick.com

A brand new magazine edited by Mike Resnick. Columns by Gregory Benford and Barry Malzberg. A mix of new and old stories.

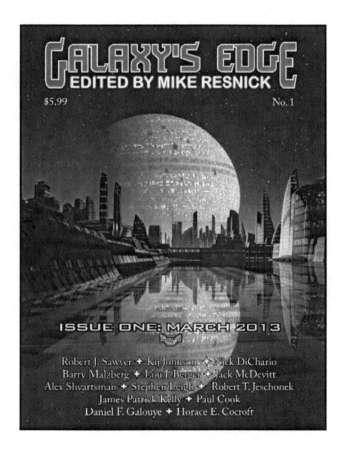

www.GalaxysEdge.com